Orcas Island

Mystery

To order additional copies of *Orcas Island Mystery*, by
Jan G. Johnson, call 1-800-765-6955.

Visit us at www.rhpa.org for more information on
Review and Herald products.

Jan G. Johnson

REVIEW AND HERALD® PUBLISHING ASSOCIATION
HAGERSTOWN, MD 21740

This book was
Edited by Gerald Wheeler
Cover design by GenesisDesign
Cover illustration by Art Landerman
Typeset: 11/14 Veljovic Book

PRINTED IN U.S.A.

02 01 00 99 98   5 4 3 2 1

R&H Cataloging Service
Johnson, Jan G.
    Orcas Island Mystery.

I. Title.
                813.54

ISBN 0-8280-1314-4

Dedication

For Cheryl and Wendy.

It isn't the destination,
but the journey.

Contents

CHAPTER 1

A Theft Aboard the Ferry

Julian and his twin sister, ReAnn, stood on the forward deck of the Washington State ferry and watched as the crew prepared the ship for departure. An air horn blasted a throaty warning, and from somewhere deep within the belly of the vessel, diesel engines vibrated to life and churned the salt water. A cloud of gulls lifted off the pier and screamed as they circled over the bay, and the ferry, the length of a football field, eased away from the dock. As Julian filled his lungs with the tangy salt air, it bit at his throat like lemonade.

He loved the smell of the sea, the cries of the gull, the blare of the horn, and the vibration of the ship under his feet. Something about it excited him. Maybe it was the fact that he and his sister were on their way to help their grandparents repair their newly purchased home on Orcas Island. Or that they were on their own while on board the ferry. Or simply because it was the beginning of summer, an opportunity for adventure.

ReAnn covered her ears and hunched her shoulders

as the horn blasted again, but not Julian. Instead, he waved to his father who stood on the dock. His dad waved in return and grew steadily smaller as the ship headed into the bay.

The horn fell silent, and ReAnn yelled, "Goodbye!"

"Do you have to scream?" her brother asked, rubbing his temples. He was sure her voice topped a hundred decibels.

"Oh, look," she exclaimed excitedly, pointing toward a large bird, flying low over the water.

"It's an eagle," Julian observed. He hunched his shoulders against the early morning chill as the ship turned into the wind.

"A bald eagle," ReAnn corrected, her blond hair trailing behind her. "Do you know what that means?"

Her brother made a face. "I can't imagine."

"It's a fortuitous event." ReAnn seemed to love big words. Julian thought she used them just to irritate him.

"I suppose it's an Indian thing."

"Native American, you mean. Yes, coastal tribes thought that sighting one at the beginning of a journey was a good thing."

"It's just a bird," he said dryly.

"A raven is 'just a bird' too, but it brought food to Elijah. It kept him from starvation."

"Well, I'm starving." Because they had left their Seattle home early in order to catch the 8:00 ferry, they hadn't eaten breakfast. The rumble in Julian's stomach reminded him of that fact. "I doubt that eagle is going to feed us." He turned toward the cabin.

"It would if God told it to." ReAnn trailed after her brother. "Maybe it's a sign."

"Yeah, sure."

"No, really. Like maybe we're coming to an intersection. You know, where paths diverge."

"Diverge?"

"It means to branch."

"I know what it means," Julian said with exasperation. "I just wondered where you were going with this."

"If paths diverge, we must take one or the other. Isn't that true? Once we do, maybe our lives will never be the same."

Julian paused at the door to the cabin. "Now let me see. Here's the choice: I could stay out here in this wind, get hypothermia, catch pneumonia, and ruin my summer. Or I could follow the path through this door, get warm, have breakfast, and live forever."

"No one lives forever." She giggled.

"Elijah did, didn't he?" Pulling open the door, Julian walked into the cabin.

Finding a lunch counter amidships, the brother and sister waited in a short line of people and selected their food items from under the protective sheets of glass. Julian thought of it as a modern version of hunting and gathering, an expression his eighth-grade teacher had used to describe the Native Americans prior to the European migration. He grabbed a chocolate-covered donut and a caffeine-free cola soft drink.

"You're going to rot your insides," ReAnn said with a frown. She selected a banana and container of orange juice.

"If I were a monkey, I'd eat bananas." He pulled a bill out of his wallet and waited for the girl ahead of him to finish paying for her food. He guessed her to be no more than 10 years old.

"You're 48 cents short," the cashier said in a tone that could cut stone. The girl looked down at the food on her paper plate, and as she did, her shoulder-length black hair fell forward over her face. "You'll have to put something back," the woman added.

"My mom has more money," the girl said, barely above a whisper.

"I don't have time to wait," the cashier said. "Put something back now. You can buy more later, if you like."

Julian felt his sister poke him in the ribs, and over his shoulder he heard her whisper, "Do something."

"Do what?" he hissed back.

The younger girl reached for an orange.

"That's only 40 cents," the cashier said. "What else?"

The girl placed the orange back on her plate and next selected a blueberry muffin and set it on the counter.

"Pay the 48 cents," ReAnn whispered to her brother. She jabbed him this time.

"Ouch," he muttered. The girl and the cashier looked at him, the girl smiling nervously. Julian cleared his throat. "I think I have enough to pay for all of us." He handed the cashier the money and frowned at his sister. Without a word, the cashier rang up the total and gave Julian the change.

"Thank you for the help," the black-haired girl said as they walked toward the observation deck. "My mom will pay you back." She paused before a display of brochures featuring Northwest tourist attractions. "Here," she said, handing him one.

"The Rainy Day Bookstore, the best selection on

Orcas Island," the leaflet announced.

"It's the *only* bookstore on the island," the girl said, "and my mom owns it." The center of the brochure contained a photo of two men huddled over a chessboard surrounded by shelves of books. "I'm the inventory manager, my mom says," the girl added. "That means I shelve books. It's my job after school. Come on, I'll show you where my mom is."

As Julian and ReAnn followed the girl into a large seating area, the ferry shuddered as it crossed the wake of a passing ship. For a moment Julian felt the floor slip beneath him, and his grip tightened around his soft drink.

"I don't know why the cashier was being so difficult," the girl continued. "We have a till in the bookstore just like the one she was using, and we can have two transactions going at the same time."

"Maybe she just didn't want to be bothered," ReAnn replied.

"My guess is she's been stung by other customers," Julian said, "and it has made her suspicious."

"It happens," the girl commented. "My mom watches customers all the time. Not the island people, you understand, but the off-islanders like him." She pointed toward a man sleeping on a bench seat next to the window. An oil-canvas overcoat, tattered around the sleeves and deeply soiled, was pulled around his neck. His long greasy hair fell over his bearded face and swept the floor. At his feet lay a dog, a black labrador retriever. It raised its head as the three passed and watched them with its one good eye. The other was only an empty socket, and an ugly flap of skin hung under its eye and pulled the lip away from its teeth, which gave the animal an angry, fierce appearance.

Julian quickened his pace.

"What a hideous dog," ReAnn said after they were safely past.

"So is the man," the girl added. "Did you see the scar on his face? No telling what he'd steal." Julian didn't remember seeing a scar. "My name is Allie," the girl continued. "Do you live on the islands? I don't remember seeing you."

"My name is ReAnn Hunter, and this is my brother, Julian. We're visiting our grandparents for the summer. They live on Orcas Island."

"They do? We'll see each other often then. What's their name?"

"Will . . . ," Julian began.

"Willard," ReAnn interrupted. "Willard is his real name, but he goes by Will."

"Thanks for that update," Julian groaned.

"Annotation," ReAnn added. "It was really an annotation."

"Whatever," he muttered. "Like I was saying before I was interrupted. . . ." ReAnn giggled. "Will and Marion Hunter are their names."

"They just retired to the island, coming from California," ReAnn put in.

"I don't think I know them, but lots of retired people move to the island. I was born there."

"How about your parents?" Julian asked.

"They moved to the island after they got married. My dad works for the state park service, and a few years ago my mother opened the bookstore. By the way, which of you is older? I've been trying to figure it out, but I can't."

"I am," Julian said, "by 30 minutes."

Allie looked puzzled. "Thirty minutes?"

"We're twins," ReAnn explained, "but you'd think 30 minutes were 10 years."

"I *am* older," Julian protested.

"Of course you are," ReAnn replied, "and shorter." Her brother groaned again. Turning to Allie, ReAnn added, "Somehow it makes him feel important to know he's older."

Allie looked from one twin to the other, then said, "You sort of look alike, I guess."

"We're fraternal twins," Julian said, rolling his eyes. "We don't have to look alike."

"I wish I had a sister or brother my age," Allie sighed. "Having a twin would be really cool."

"It has its moments," ReAnn smiled.

"Very few," Julian mumbled.

"It's fine as long as parents don't dress us the same," ReAnn added.

Julian groaned once more as he remembered photos of them as babies wearing the same outfit.

Allie laughed. "I could see that."

"It's hard enough being a twin without always being compared," Julian moaned. He plopped onto the nearest chair and popped open the tab on his can of soft drink. "I'm hungry and want to eat. Besides, the conversation is getting boring."

"Come on," ReAnn coaxed. "No one meant to make you angry."

"I surely didn't," Allie agreed.

Julian shook his head and gulped his soft drink. The fizz tickled his nose and bit at his throat.

"Let's go meet Allie's mother," ReAnn said. "You like books. It might be a good idea to get on the good side of a bookstore owner."

"I would rather be by myself." He took a husky bite of his donut. Putting it back onto the paper plate, he noticed that he'd gotten chocolate on his fingers. He licked it off.

ReAnn shrugged, and the two girls continued walking.

"Touchy, isn't he?" Julian heard Allie ask.

"You don't know the half of it," his sister said.

The two girls continued talking and moved beyond Julian's hearing.

Stuffing the napkin into his shirt pocket and taking his drink in one hand and his donut in the other, he jumped up and jogged after them, leaving the plate behind.

"OK," he said, "but no more of that dress-up talk."

"Wouldn't think of it," ReAnn said with a smile.

Allie's mother, Mrs. Maggie Freewall, was a lanky woman with short black hair salted with gray. She removed her reading glasses as they approached, closed her book, and placed it on her lap. After listening to Allie's story about the money and how Julian had come to her aid, she said, "That was really thoughtful of you, Julian."

"It was nothing," he said. He looked down at his donut and realized the icing had somehow smeared his fingers again.

"Why don't you sit down and finish your breakfast, and when you're done, I'll pay you back."

"Thank you," ReAnn said, taking a seat immediately.

Julian reluctantly joined his sister although he'd rather eat alone. Balancing his donut on the lid of the pop can, he fished his napkin out of his pocket and wiped his fingers.

"Julian and ReAnn are twins," Allie announced. She peeled the cellophane away from her blueberry muffin and began to eat the muffin.

"What's it like to be in the same classroom?" Mrs. Freewall asked.

"It's great," ReAnn answered. She had neatly peeled back the skin on her banana and was slowly eating the white flesh. "I'm good at physics and chemistry, and Julian likes history. He quizzes me for our history tests, and I helped him with his science project." She took another bite.

"I also do your book reports," Julian added. Studying his donut, he decided it was beginning to look as if it had been through a war.

"One report," ReAnn said defensively. "I couldn't finish *The Red Badge of Courage*. Not enough conversation."

"I see," Mrs. Freewall said.

Julian placed his can of pop on the floor and balanced the donut on it.

"You're not hungry?" Allie asked him.

"It's probably sea queasiness," Mrs. Freewall suggested. "Not enough to make you vomit, but enough to turn your gills green. Does your stomach feel as if it's about to roll over?"

Now that she mentioned it, Julian noticed his stomach did feel as if he'd just gotten off a roller coaster. He nodded.

"It's probably the pop," ReAnn said. "On an empty stomach, it can't be good for him."

Julian thought he might walk around the cabin for a while. Maybe it would help him feel better. The boat shuddered and slipped sideways as it rounded the end of

17

an island. Julian's stomach bounced too.

Allie popped the remaining muffin into her mouth and washed it down with milk. ReAnn rolled the banana skin into a napkin and drained her orange juice. Mrs. Freewall wiped a bead of juice from the corner of her mouth after biting down on a wedge of orange.

Feeling that he suddenly needed to get some fresh air, Julian stood and started toward the door that led to the bow.

"Wait, Julian," Mrs. Freewall said. "I have 48 cents right here." She reached under her coat for her purse but found nothing. "Where's my purse?" she asked absently, removing her coat from the seat. The purse wasn't there. "It's got to be here," she insisted, panic building in her voice. Dropping to her knees, she peered under the seat.

Julian noticed the stranger sit up, push his dog to the side, and stand. He stretched his lanky limbs and slipped into his canvas coat. It fell loosely around his body to his legs.

Mrs. Freewall jerked to her feet and exclaimed, "Someone took my purse!" The stranger walked toward amidships, his dog trailing at his heels with its tail drooping.

CHAPTER 2

A
Near Miss

An hour later, Julian and his sister pushed their bikes off the ferry and up the ramp onto Orcas Island. Grandpa, dressed in a red flannel shirt and blue jeans, stood at the head of the ramp, waving and calling to them.

Mrs. Freewall drove past in an ancient moss-green Volvo and tapped her horn. Allie waved from the open window, and called, "Come and see me."

ReAnn waved in return.

A county sheriff, a tall Black man dressed in a pressed uniform with a colorful Island County insignia on his sleeve, stood at the cross streets and directed some of the cars toward a parking area. Mrs. Freewall's car was one of them. Along the hill a line of cars waited with engines idling to board the ferry.

"I'm so glad to see you," Grandpa said, engulfing first one twin and then the other in his burly arms. He planted a kiss on Julian's forehead. "This is going to be a great summer. I'm so glad you're here."

"Me, too," ReAnn said.

"Hey, you two," the sheriff called. He pointed toward the twins. "I want to talk to you. Pull your bikes into the parking lot."

"What's this all about?" Grandpa asked, his bushy eyebrows knitted in an expression of concern above his bifocals.

"There was a theft aboard the ferry," Julian explained. "I think he wants to question us."

"You're suspects?" Grandpa asked. "My grandchildren are suspects!"

"No," ReAnn said. "We were with Mrs. Freewall when she discovered her purse was missing."

As grandpa put the twins' bikes and gear into his Toyota pickup, he asked numerous questions. Julian and ReAnn told how they had helped Allie purchase her breakfast and how they had met Mrs. Freewall.

"Do you know her?" ReAnn asked. "She owns the bookstore."

Julian handed grandpa the brochure Allie had given him. Opening it, Grandpa paused at the photo of the two men playing chess. "I know these guys," he said. "This is Pastor John Bright of the Community Church, and the other is Father Trudeau. They are on my 'must see' list. If you want something done, you've got to talk to the right people, you know." He handed the brochure back to Julian.

After they had the gear secured in the pickup, Grandpa and the twins joined a small group of people waiting in the parking lot. The stranger in the canvas coat leaned against a rock retaining wall with arms crossed, his dog curled at his feet. A bike with worn packs called panniers leaned against the wall next to him. Articles of clothing carelessly stuffed under bungee cords hung from the panniers, and a single fiberglass pole, with a tattered orange flag attached to it, rose over the rear wheel.

"Was Mrs. Freewall carrying a lot of money in her purse?" Grandpa asked.

"Eighty dollars or so," Julian said. "But it wasn't the money she was worried about as much as her mother's wedding ring."

"She had taken it to a jeweler in Anacortes," ReAnn added. "She had the diamond reset and the ring cleaned."

"It's a sentimental thing, I guess," Julian commented.

"How do you know the purse was stolen?" Grandpa asked.

"Mrs. Freewall thought it was stolen the moment she couldn't find it," he said.

The sheriff finished questioning Mrs. Freewall, snapped shut a small spiral notebook, and waved the stranger over to him. Mrs. Freewall turned her Volvo onto the road and disappeared around a corner.

"We looked everywhere," ReAnn explained. "The restroom, Mrs. Freewall's car, the cabin area, every place she could remember she'd been. It has to be stolen."

The long line of cars, waiting to board, began moving down the pier onto the ferry. The ramp made a rhythmic clanking sound as cars drove over it.

"Lost or stolen," Grandpa said. "It has to be one or the other."

The stranger rolled his bike to a stop in front of the sheriff.

"Or discarded," Julian suggested.

"You honestly don't think Mrs. Freewall threw away her own purse and then claimed it had been stolen?" ReAnn asked.

"I didn't say I thought that," her brother protested. "I was just trying to think of all the alternatives."

"Well, think of another," ReAnn said. "That one doesn't make sense. Why would she do it?"

"That's a question of motivation," Grandpa said. "Every crime is committed by someone who has motivation. Take Julian's idea. What motivation would cause her to throw it overboard and then claim that it was stolen?"

"Insurance?" the boy asked.

"Maybe. A mother's wedding ring may be worth more sentimentally than it's worth in cash. But you get the idea. People don't just act randomly. They do things because of some reason."

"Well, whether it makes sense or not," Julian said, folding his arms across his chest, "it's certainly an alternative."

"It makes about as much sense to say that Allie took the purse," ReAnn said with disgust.

"If it were stolen, she'd be a suspect," Julian replied.

"If you want a suspect," she said, "consider that guy." The stranger pulled a wallet from his hip pocket, removed his driver's license, and handed it to the sheriff. "He's more likely the thief than Allie. Allie didn't have enough money to pay for her breakfast, or did you forget?"

The sheriff copied something into his notebook and handed the license back. The stranger placed the card in his wallet and opened the wallet for the sheriff's inspection. After replacing his wallet in his pocket, the man submitted to a search. After patting him down, the sheriff pawed through the panniers. Apparently finding nothing, the police officer waved the stranger on. The man threw his leg over his bike and pedaled slowly up the hill, his dog trotting alongside.

The sheriff circulated among the remaining cars, taking names and addresses. Finally, leaning against the door of his police cruiser, he waved Julian and ReAnn over to him. He jotted more notes in his book as they approached.

"Were you the two who were with Mrs. Freewall when she discovered her purse was missing?" he asked.

"Yes," Julian said.

"My name is Sheriff Mike Jordan," he said, extending his hand. Julian shook it.

"I'm Will Hunter," Grandpa added, shaking the sheriff's hand, too. "My wife and I bought the Brightwood home and moved in a few months ago."

"Yeah, I heard someone took over the old place." The policeman wrote a quick note in his book. "Welcome to the county. You know these kids?"

The ferry's horn bellowed, signaling the boat was about to depart.

"They're my grandchildren."

"Are you planning to be here for a while?" the sheriff asked after he got their names and recorded them in his book.

"For the summer," Julian told him.

"Then I'll know where to find you," he said. He settled into his cruiser, inserted his key into the ignition, and turned it. The car's starter whined, but the engine refused to catch. The officer pumped the gas and tried again.

The ferry's horn sounded a second time, and two boys raced down the hill from the upper parking lot. Their feet hit the pavement with resounding slaps, and as they passed the police cruiser, one of the boys slapped his hands against the car's hood. "Get a horse," he shouted as he and his taller friend continued running toward the ferry. "It would have more get up and go."

"Hey!" the sheriff shouted. "Keep your hands to yourself."

"Sorry," the shorter boy said. Both boys laughed and lunged down the pier, leaping onto the ferry as the ramp lifted off the dock. Water churned, and the ferry began backing out into the channel.

"You'd be smart not to have anything to do with those two," the sheriff said. "They're trouble. Both of them have too much time on their hands."

Once on deck, the taller boy playfully punched the other on the shoulder. The other pushed the first, and dashed into the stairway that led to the upper deck. Letting out a whoop, the taller boy followed.

"What about the man with the dog?" Julian asked.

"Cat Billet?" the sheriff asked. "He's a gnat's eyelash away from being a vagrant. A $10 bill rolled up in the corner of his wallet prevents me from arresting him. We get a lot of his type during the summer. Little or no money and nowhere to go. He'll probably camp in Moran State Park for the 14-day limit, and then we'll kick him out. I'll keep my eye on him though."

The two boys on the ferry stood in the wind on the upper deck as the ship turned toward San Juan Island.

"Do you think this Mr. Billet stole the purse?" ReAnn asked.

"Could have, but it's not on him now," Sheriff Jordan said. "But if he's a thief, we'll catch him."

Grandpa and the twins returned to the pickup. Across the parking lot, the sheriff continued to crank his engine. Grandpa checked the bikes a final time, then slid behind the wheel of his pickup and asked, "Seat belts on?"

"Yes," the twins chimed together.

"Good," he said. He started his pickup with a flick of his key and turned toward the sheriff's car.

"Can I help?" Grandpa asked as he pulled alongside.

"Only a new patrol car would help," the sheriff said and slammed the flat of his hand against the steering wheel. "Maybe the commissioners will budget for one next year. But let me tell you, if they had to drive this heap, they'd replace it immediately. Politics!" The last word exploded as if it were a red-hot coal burning his lips.

In the distance, the ferry turned into the channel, and the boys on the forward deck were no longer visible.

"You wouldn't know of a place where a new group of Christians could meet, do you?" Grandpa asked. "I'm trying to start a group interested in learning more about the prophecies of the Bible."

The sheriff thought a moment before responding. "Nothing comes to mind, but I'll keep my eyes open."

"Thanks," Grandpa said. "May I give you a lift?"

"You could," the sheriff said, "but then I'd have to ticket you, because one of us would not be wearing a seat belt, and it wouldn't be me."

Grandpa smiled, waved goodbye, and drove out of the parking lot.

They passed a restaurant, gift shops, and the entrance to the upper parking area before giant fir trees closed around the narrow, twisting road. The sudden darkness of the forest stood in marked contrast to the bright sunlight of the ferry landing.

"I bought paint for the house and stain for the porch and deck," Grandpa said. "I have new linoleum on order for the bathroom, and a roofer is scheduled for the end of the month. We'll let an expert do the roof."

"I like to paint," Julian volunteered. He rolled down the window and enjoyed the feel of the cool air. "Does the house need scraping?"

"I've already done it, and it's primed." Grandpa slowed his pickup for a sharp curve. Limbs, heavy with needles, hung low over the road. "It won't be all work, though. There'll be plenty of time for play and for another project I'm working on. With God's blessing, I'm going to start an Adventist church on the island, and you're going to help me."

"We are?" ReAnn said with excitement.

"We've got to give literature to as many people as we can before our first meeting," Grandpa said.

"When will that be?" Julian asked.

"This Saturday," Grandpa explained. "I'm starting a prophecy study group in order to build interest. Those wanting to join the church will later become a part of a group called a company."

"All right!" ReAnn exclaimed.

"Won't that be fun," Julian said under his breath.

ReAnn jabbed him with her elbow.

A large animal jumped from the shadows at the side of the road into Grandpa's path. Grandpa swerved to miss it and hit the brakes. Julian felt the pickup slide, and the tires squealed against the asphalt. Outside Julian's window waved an orange flag on the end of a fiberglass pole. Julian was sure he could have reached out and touched it.

CHAPTER 3

The
Mystery Deepens

The pickup slid to a stop broadside in the road. A black lab, the animal Grandpa narrowly missed, trotted past Julian's side of the pickup, its red tongue drooping. Cat Billet continued pedaling his bike down the road without looking back. Dressed in his dark trench coat, he looked more shadowlike than human.

Grandpa's house sat at the end of a winding lane surrounded by fir trees and looked out on East Sound, a neck of water that nearly sliced Orcas Island in half. White primer spotted the forest-green paint on his house, and the redwood front porch, checked and gray with age, spanned the width of the house.

Grandma pushed past a screen door and stood on the porch, beaming. She was mixing something in a basketball-sized plastic bowl held in her left arm, and what looked like flour spotted her violet blouse. She put the bowl on the porch and dashed across the lawn toward them.

"I'm so glad to see you," she said. Throwing her

arms around her grandchildren, she pressed them to her chest. Julian brushed the flour off his shirt after she released him. "Oh, my. I didn't realize I'd made such a mess of myself." She flicked at the flour stains with the back of her hand. "I'm mixing wallpaper paste."

"Oh, yes," Grandpa said from the back of the pickup. He grunted as he pulled the twins' duffel bags from the box. "We're also hanging wallpaper. Have either of you done that before?"

"No," the twins replied in unison.

"Well, never mind," he said, heading for the house. "You'll learn soon enough."

While Grandma went to the kitchen to fix lunch, Grandpa showed the twins to their rooms. Julian's room faced the water. He could hear the cry of seagulls through his open window. ReAnn's bedroom was across the hall. It looked out on the front porch and the trees beyond. Julian decided his room was perfect.

After a lunch of reheated pizza and watermelon, the twins helped hang wallpaper in the master bedroom and living room. Julian and his grandma cut the paper and brushed paste on the back while his sister and grandpa positioned the long strips and brushed out the air bubbles. Several hours later, they relaxed on the deck with a pitcher of fresh lemonade and watched the late afternoon sun play on the water.

"I think that's about all the work for today." Grandpa drained his glass and continued, "I want to work on the invitation for the study group I'm starting."

"He just wants to get back to his computer," Grandma said, smiling broadly. "He's become quite a hacker."

"What's a hacker?" Grandpa asked. "Isn't that some-one with a cough?"

"Can I help?" ReAnn asked. "I have some ideas you might like to try."

"Sure." The two disappeared into the house.

Grandma collected the glasses and hummed to her-self as she washed them in the kitchen.

Julian leaned back in his chair and stared out onto the bay. A gentle breeze rippled the water in a southerly direction, giving the water the appearance of move-ment. He remembered the uncomfortable feeling he had in his stomach while aboard the ferry. Had he been seasick like Mrs. Freewall had suggested? Or was his stomach simply upset because of his junk-food break-fast? He hoped it wasn't because of seasickness. He liked the water and would like to spend more time on it. Liking junk food, too, he doubted that it would rot his in-sides like his sister had said.

Before going to bed that night, Grandpa and ReAnn proudly showed the invitation they'd worked on. Run off on a color printer, the invitation had a white-robed fig-ure standing over a man writing on a scroll. A message above the illustration read, "Prophecy Study Group: Finding Our Place in Time."

Julian thumbed the sheet front to back. The meeting place remained blank.

"It's perfect," ReAnn said with enthusiasm. "Small, easy to read, and great graphics. After we add the loca-tion, we can hand these out to everyone on the island."

Julian handed the copy back to ReAnn and slipped down the hall to his bedroom. Not enthusiastic about the project, he wondered if he could help his grandfather in some other way. It made him feel uncomfortable when well-meaning people handed him pamphlets on the street, and he figured many others felt the same way. Now he was being asked to do it, too.

The next morning, Julian entered the kitchen and discovered to his surprise that his sister had already eaten breakfast and had gone outdoors. Julian grabbed a glass of juice and was about to dash out the door when his grandma called him back and gave him two loaves of fresh-baked bread and two invitations to take to the neighbors. She said Mr. Holland lived in the cabin to the north, and that he had been lonely since the death of his wife last winter. On the bluff to the south a local artist, Rachael Falling Leaf, produced sculptures of animals in demand by collectors all over the Northwest.

"It won't do any good to hand them out," Julian protested as he accepted the invitations and bread. "We don't have a place to meet yet."

"You left last night while we were still discussing the project. We decided to put our phone number on the back and start handing them out right away."

"Oh," Julian said with a shrug. He stuffed the two pieces of paper into his pocket and pushed his way out the door. Pausing on the deck, he gulped down the juice while listening for his sister. He heard a familiar peel of laughter beyond the woods to his left. After depositing the empty glass on the picnic table, he ran into the forest toward the sound. The ground fell away rapidly, and the woods opened around a cabin at the edge of the bay.

"This is my brother," ReAnn said as Julian stepped onto the deck at the back of the house. Two adults sat in chairs talking to ReAnn.

"I'm Brent Holland," the old man introduced himself. A neat fringe of gray hair circled the top of his head, and his bushy eyebrows lifted as he leaned toward Julian. "And this woman," he added with a toss of his head, "is my dead wife's nurse, Linda Phillips. She must not know that my wife has gone, because she keeps coming around."

"Just to check on you," Linda said, patting the old man on the shoulder. A small woman, her hand looked like a child's next to the man's thick neck and wide slumping shoulders.

"Well, you're wasting your time," Mr. Holland said. He leaned back in his chair and pressed a cap onto his head. "What's in your hand, son? Are you going to feed the gulls?"

"Oh," Julian said, realizing he'd forgotten about the bread. "My grandma baked this and thought you might like some. It's fresh."

"You don't say." The old man took the bread. "Don't know what I'll do with it. Had a loaf once. It grew a nice crop of green moss." He looked toward the bay, licked his lips, and added matter-of-factly, "Then I threw it away."

"The least you could do is thank the boy," Linda Phillips said with a twinkle in her eye.

Mr. Holland dismissed her with a flick of his wrist. "Did you see the sea otters this morning? You have to get up at dawn. They swim into the kelp bed and dive for oysters. Then they lie on their backs with the water glistening on their oiled fur and break oysters on rocks they've balanced on their chests." He pointed into the morning light reflecting off the water's surface and said, "Over there is where you'll see them if you don't sleep your opportunity away. Before my skiff sunk in a storm last spring, I could drift within a hundred feet of them. Sometimes they'd circle my skiff and chatter away as if trying to talk to me. I'm sure they thought my skiff was just one great big log and me a log-bound animal."

Mr. Holland fell silent, the kind of silence in which Julian felt he shouldn't intrude. Only the sounds of nature broke into it: the wind in the trees, the cry of a distant hawk—perhaps an osprey—the rustle of a squirrel in nearby leaves, and the lap of waves on the beach.

Brian searched the waters for any sign of sea otters eating oysters directly from the shell but saw nothing.

"How about seals hunting?" Mr. Holland said finally. "Have you seen them? I have. I saw a couple of Canadian geese on the beach earlier. Did you know they mate for life? For life."

More silence followed.

"I've got to go," Linda said finally. "There's a sick person on the other side of the island who really needs my attention." She squeezed the old man's hand, and when she let go, it fell limply to his lap.

Linda motioned to the twins to follow her. As she stepped off the deck, she picked up a bottle that had apparently fallen from the deck and threw it into the garbage can. Together they walked to her car. "I appreciate your visiting Mr. Holland," she said, opening the door to her bright-red Geo Metro. "He's lonely since his wife died, and it's not good for him to be alone. You'll visit him again?"

"Sure," ReAnn said.

"He's a wonderful person—he really is. His grieving has changed him. Makes him seem distant, but it's just a front, I think. Maybe it'll pass."

As Julian and ReAnn climbed the hill to the bluff where the artist lived, ReAnn said, "Sad to think a couple will live their whole life together and then one of them is gone."

"I suppose," Julian said.

"You can see how he hurts, can't you?"

"I guess."

"Maybe that's why he's drinking too much."

"What are you talking about?" Julian asked.

"Didn't you see the bottle? It contained alcohol. Not the weak stuff, either."

Julian thought about the invitation in his pocket. On the one hand, he wished he'd given it to Mr. Holland, but on the other, he cringed at the thought of it. What if the old man didn't want to be bothered?

The twins found Rachael Falling Leaf laboring over a makeshift table. Several large lumps of clay sat next to her, and her hands worked at a fourth one. From Rachael's position high on the bluff, no trees obstructed her view of East Sound. The blue water stretched from the town at the head of the bay—called Eastsound—to Blakely Island. Beyond Blakely Island, large ships passed through the straits on their way to Seattle. Directly across the bay, Mount Constitution, the highest point on Orcas Island, rose more than 2,400 feet.

After introductions, ReAnn said, "What a nice name—Falling Leaf."

"It's my Indian name," the woman said, her long braid weaving like a snake down her back as she hovered over a mound of clay. The braid, black as charcoal, reached to her knees. "I'm a Muckleshoot. My tribe lives in the foothills of the Cascades, but I live here because it's closer to the sea." Her fingers worked the clay, creating humps and valleys, squeezing the moist mass, forming shapes. "There's the shape of an orcas in this piece of clay," she said. "My fingers are searching for it."

She palmed the back of the clay and an arch emerged along the spine. A few minutes later, a head began to take shape.

"It looks easy," ReAnn said.

"It is." Rachael nudged a ball of clay toward ReAnn. "Try it."

ReAnn began working the gray material. After several minutes, she said, "It's stiffer than I thought it would be. How do you get the clay to shape so easily?"

"What shape is in your clay?" the woman asked.

"I don't know. I thought I'd work on it a while and something would emerge."

"You've got to see it first. Nothing happens if there's no vision."

ReAnn stepped back and watched Rachael work. The orca was nearly finished. More than just the shape of a killer whale, it somehow seemed real.

Finally, the woman stood back. "It's done."

"It's beautiful," ReAnn exclaimed. "How do you know when it's done?"

"When there's nothing further to do. Only a fire is needed to give it a permanence that'll last many lifetimes."

"It's awesome," Julian said.

"Then it's yours," Rachael said with a broad smile.

"Oh, no," Julian said. "I couldn't take it."

"You've seen its creation. It's yours already."

For several moments, Julian admired the sculpture. He wished he could take it now.

"I nearly forgot," he said, suddenly remembering the bread. "We brought you a loaf of my grandma's bread. I mean, she asked me to. But it doesn't seem like a fair trade."

"Very fair," Rachael said. "One creative gift for another. Now, let's eat fresh bread and elderberry jelly and seal the exchange."

Rachael led the twins into her cabin. Constructed of logs with a pine floor, the house had large windows that opened toward the sea. They were divided into dozens of small panes, and a large fireplace made of river rock occupied the middle of the wall. A small fire burned on the hearth, and the room smelled of wood smoke. The stone above the fireplace had blackened from years of fires.

They sat at Rachael's table before the window that viewed the bay. As they ate thick slices of bread with generous layers of jelly, Rachael told of a kayak adventure in which she and a dozen Eskimos had hunted seal in Alaska and found themselves surrounded by a pod of killer whales.

"They often travel in groups," she explained, "and are like families. I still hear their song. It comes to me at night, and in the morning I'm ready to look for them again in my clay. It's as if they live inside me. My fingers transfer them to the clay, and I work with it until they appear."

She looked out the window and raised her arms above her head. Opening her mouth, she began to chant. Her body swayed to the music, and her braid followed her body, reminding Julian of moving water.

"They followed us for hours," she then continued quietly. "Surfacing around our kayaks, they blew water into the air and sang their songs."

"Weren't you afraid?" ReAnn asked.

"I was afraid that I wouldn't see all there was to see and hear all there was to hear," Rachael answered. "Sometimes fear makes us blind and deaf."

After they had washed and put away the dishes, Julian and ReAnn were preparing to leave when an invitation slipped from Julian's pocket.

"What's this?" ReAnn asked as she reached for it.

"It's . . . well, I . . . ," Julian stammered.

"It's an invitation," ReAnn said, looking first at the paper in her hand and then at her brother.

"Yes," he said sheepishly.

"An invitation?" Rachael asked.

"Yes. It's for people wanting to know about God's word." ReAnn handed the paper to the woman, but she glared at her brother.

"Is this something new?" Rachael asked.

"We don't even know where it'll be held," ReAnn said. "But we'll find some place soon. Would you like me to let you know when we find a place?"

"It never hurts to know more about God," the sculptor replied.

As they walked down the hill, ReAnn ignored her brother. Julian alternated between wishing she would say something and hoping she wouldn't.

"Give me the other one," she said when they reached the bottom of the hill.

Julian handed it to her. Grabbing it with a snap, she disappeared into the woods, heading in the direction of Mr. Holland's home. Julian kicked at the dirt and turned toward home.

After working on their grandparent's house all morning, the twins rode their bikes into the town of Eastsound. They wanted to see if there was any news about the missing purse.

As they entered town, a boy Julian recognized as one of the two the sheriff had warned them about slipped through a hedge and watched them as they approached.

"Saw you at the ferry landing yesterday," he said as the twins drew near. He thrust his thumbs carelessly into his Levi's pockets.

Julian's bike tire slid in the loose rock at the side of the road as he pulled to a stop. "Saw you too," he said.

"You're new here?"

"My sister and I are staying with our grandparents," Julian said.

"Will and Marian Hunter," ReAnn added.

"Uh, huh. Wonderful." He yawned. It seemed deliberate to Julian. "I'm Rand Andrews," he announced. "The other guy you saw was my brother, Jay."

"My name's Julian, and this is my sister, ReAnn."

"You staying here long?"

"The summer. We're helping my grandparents repair their house."

"We'll see you around then. There isn't much going on around here. For a little action, we take the ferry to Friday Harbor. It's the next ferry stop. The town's all right when there aren't too many tourists around."

"Is that where you were headed yesterday?"

"Yeah. We saw a movie. Maybe you'd like to come sometime."

"Maybe," Julian said. "Where's the bookstore?"

"Follow your nose," he said. "You can't miss it." He turned back into the hedge and disappeared.

Julian and his sister continued down the street. Rainy Day Bookstore was a single-story building at the edge of the bay. An alley between the bookstore and a restaurant led to a pier. An old skiff needing a coat of paint bobbed next to a piling at the end of the pier. A fisherman sat beside it on a three-legged stool, his pole on the dock next to him.

The twins leaned their bikes against the wall in the alley and entered the store through a hand-carved door. Fir trees, birds, deer, and bear stood out in bold relief on the door panels and were polished with oil. A bell above the door rang, and someone immediately yelped a greeting in the back of the store.

"I wondered if you'd come," Allie said, jogging up the aisle.

A display of books at the door caught Julian's attention. One titled *Pacific Sea Otters* rested in a plastic display holder with the face of a furry creature looking up at him. Julian picked it up and thumbed through it.

"Wouldn't miss it," ReAnn said as Allie approached. "Hear anything about your mother's purse?"

"Hey, look at this," Julian interrupted. He opened the book toward his sister. A map showing the distribution of the sea otter in the Pacific Ocean indicated concentrations only along the central California coast and in the waters off Alaska.

"What about it?" ReAnn asked. Allie looked at the book too.

"According to this, there are no sea otters in the San Juan archipelago," Julian explained.

"I've never seen any," Allie commented.

"Mr. Holland said he's seen them," ReAnn said.

38

"He may have seen something, but he hasn't seen any sea otters." Julian replaced the book.

"Come on," Allie said. "I'll show you the store."

"What about your mother's purse?" ReAnn asked a second time.

"Nothing," Allie told her, "but the sheriff said he has some leads."

"Good," Julian said. "I hope he finds it."

As they walked through the store, Allie pointed out the categories of books. Mrs. Freewall, talking on the phone, waved to them as they passed her counter. In the back of the store the windows opened onto the sound. At a table, two men sat playing chess. They were the same two men Julian remembered seeing pictured in the brochure.

"These are the friends I was telling you about," Allie said as she introduced the twins.

Pastor John Bright smiled and said, "This is the Orcas Island ministerial meeting."

The Catholic priest, Father Trudeau, nodded in agreement. "If it weren't for this meeting, we'd have no meetings at all."

"Don't let him fool you," Pastor Bright said. "We get a lot of work done between checkmates." Pastor Bright moved his queen across the board and said, "Checkmate."

Father Trudeau bent over the board and lifted his glasses onto his forehead.

A shout came from the front of the store. Both twins turned at once and saw Mrs. Freewall holding up a brown leather purse. "It's back," she exclaimed. "Someone returned my purse."

39

CHAPTER 4

Wind in Her Hair

Patrons quickly gathered at the counter as Maggie Freewall scattered the contents of her purse across the polished wood surface. Her cash and credit cards were still in her billfold. She sorted through the papers until she found a plain white envelope that she cupped in her hands before opening it. A ring, her mother's, dropped onto the counter when she broke the seal.

"Can't believe it," Mrs. Freewall said, covering her mouth with her hand, not taking her eyes off the ring.

"Is anything missing?" Pastor Bright asked.

"Of course not," Father Trudeau said. "Do you think the thief would return the cash and keep her lipstick?"

"I don't use lipstick." Mrs. Freewall placed the diamond ring over the first knuckle of her index finger and watched the light bounce off the facets.

"Nail clippers, then," Father Trudeau laughed. "You do clip your nails, don't you?"

"Shouldn't someone get the sheriff?" ReAnn asked.

"Of course, I do," Mrs. Freewall said in answer to

Father Trudeau's question. She pulled a shiny pair of nail clippers out of the pile and said, "They're right here."

"I'll get him," Allie volunteered and ran out of the store.

"My point exactly," Father Trudeau said.

"Look over the contents carefully," Pastor Bright urged. "Maybe there's a clue."

"Nothing is missing," Mrs. Freewall reported after searching through the contents.

"Nothing at all?" Sheriff Jordan asked as he entered the shop. Allie shadowed close behind him.

"Not that I can tell," Mrs. Freewall answered. She scooped the contents back into her purse. "Nothing important, anyway."

"You questioned that vagrant, didn't you, Sheriff?" Pastor Bright asked. "Maybe you scared him, and he returned it."

"Where did you find your purse, Maggie?" the sheriff questioned.

"Under the counter. I was taking an order on the phone, and when I finished the conversation, I reached under the counter for the order book and found the purse instead."

"Was that the first time you looked in that spot this morning?" Mike Jordan continued.

"I think so."

The sheriff rubbed his chin. "As far as I can tell, no crime has been committed. Case closed." He headed for the door.

"Wait a minute," Pastor Bright called after him. "How do you know the thief didn't break into the store and return the purse? A break-in is still a crime, isn't it?"

The sheriff looked at Mrs. Freeland. "Did you notice any sign of a break-in, Maggie?"

"None."

Sheriff Jordan opened the door and inspected the doorjamb and lock. When finished, he shrugged and walked into the street, pulling the door closed behind him.

"Hmm." Pastor Bright ran his hand through his thick black hair. Built like a marathon runner—thin with muscles like ropes—he looked like an animal about ready to spring. "This makes me uneasy. Someone stole the purse and then returned it with all its contents. Do you suppose he got your home address and is stealing you blind while you're at work?"

"He could have done that without returning the purse," Father Trudeau suggested.

"True," Pastor Bright said, heading for the door. "But it's best to check it out."

"What about our chess game?" Father Trudeau protested.

"It'll have to wait. I've got to talk to the sheriff." Pastor Bright threw the door open and disappeared into the street.

"I'm glad you got your purse back, Maggie," Father Trudeau said. "It's a mystery—it truly is. But one with a happy ending, it appears." He placed his hat on his head and left the store.

"Could it have been returned yesterday?" Julian asked, glad finally to be able to get in a question.

"I used my order book after I closed the store last night. If my purse had been there, I would have seen it."

"If he didn't break in, he must have returned it this morning," Julian observed. "Could someone have entered the shop without your knowing it, placed the purse under the counter, and left before being seen?"

"I don't see how," Mrs. Freewall told her. She looked toward the door and added, "We installed the bell above the door to prevent that sort of thing. But how else could it have happened?"

"One more thing," Julian said. "Did Cat Billet come in the store today?"

"Who?" Mrs. Freewall asked.

"The stranger with the dog," Allie explained.

"No. I would have remembered him."

Allie accompanied the twins as they left the shop.

"Was there any time when you and your mother were not at the counter?" Julian asked.

"Sure, lots of times. We were all over the store. But how would the thief know where we were?"

The sheriff pulled himself out from under the hood of his police cruiser. After wiping his hands on a cloth, he slammed the hood. "I've got to get this bucket-of-bolts fixed. Car barely runs, and Pastor Bright wants me to make sure no one is breaking into Maggie's house. I'd forget the whole thing, but in the event he's right, unlikely though it may be, I've got to go."

Slipping behind the wheel, the sheriff turned the key. The starter whined, the engine belched, blue smoke rose from the exhaust pipe, but the engine didn't start. He tried a second time. Again a burst of blue smoke, but this time the engine coughed, sputtered, and groaned to life.

The sheriff rolled his window down and said, "Saw Rand stop you this morning in front of the Blue Pelican Resort. Was he bothering you?"

"No," the twins said.

"If he does, let me know. I'll break him. How those boys got a job at the resort, I'll never know." Sheriff Jordan sped off, blue smoke swirling behind the car.

Julian and ReAnn retrieved their bikes from the alley.

"Thank you for coming to the store," Allie said. "Will I see you again soon?"

"Soon," Julian promised. "We're in this mystery together, and we've got to keep each other updated."

"I'd like that." The girl smiled warmly, opened the door, and disappeared into the shop.

On their way out of town, the twins passed the sheriff's office. Julian noticed spray-can graffiti on the white walls. The large swirls trailed across the wall, black as night, in an indecipherable script.

As they passed the Blue Pelican Resort, Rand called to them. He ran down the lawn, his brother close behind.

"Did you find the bookstore all right?" Rand asked.

"Well, your directions got us there," Julian said sourly and stopped next to Rand. He got off his bike.

"Did I give directions?" Rand asked. "I don't remember."

"'Follow your nose,' you said."

"Oh, yeah." Rand grinned, teeth showing. "I'm glad it worked for you."

"The sheriff thought you might be giving us trouble," Julian continued. "Why would he think that?"

"I don't know," Rand replied. "Do you, Jay?"

"No idea," his brother said, shrugging his shoulders.

Julian got back on his bike.

"Wait," Rand said. "Jay and I were wondering . . . well, we were thinking you'd like to . . . I mean."

"He's not good at invitations," Jay interrupted, shoving his brother aside. "We're going kayaking Thursday.

Gray whales often feed in the kelp beds off Peapod Rocks. It's an easy trip by kayak from Doe Bay. Do you want to come?"

"Sure," Julian said. "Sounds fun."

"We'll rent kayaks at Doe Bay," Jay said.

"At Pastor Bright's shop," Rand added. "He rents cheap to locals. Maybe we can convince him to do the same for you, since you're going to be here this summer."

"Don't bet on it," Jay said. "Bring a twenty. He squeezes a dollar dry."

"Anything else?" Julian said.

"Yeah," Rand said. "The next time the sheriff asks if we're giving you a bad time, tell him yes."

"We have a reputation to keep up," Jay added.

Rand tussled Jay's hair, and the two boys chased each other up the lawn.

The twins resumed their trip home. As they silently pedaled along, Julian mulled over the strange reappearance of the purse. Could it be that the thief, afraid that he might be found out, returned the purse as Pastor Bright had suggested? But if he or she was afraid of discovery, why risk delivering it to the store? Wouldn't it be far easier and safer to throw the purse and its contents into the sea?

"Julian," ReAnn said, finally breaking the silence, "I don't understand you sometimes."

"You're just coming to that? I seldom understand you."

"Why were you rude to Rand and his brother?" Lowering her voice, she mimicked Julian, "'The sheriff thought you might be giving us trouble. Why would he think that?'" Resuming her normal voice, she said, "Man, Julian, you can be so rude sometimes."

"Rude?"

"Rude. Impolite. Bad-mannered. Boorish. Any of those. All of those."

"At least I don't embarrass people by thrusting invitations on them."

"I do not," ReAnn said, stopping her bike. "I only offer it. They don't have to take it, and they're certainly not embarrassed about it."

"Well, I am," Julian said, braking his bike to a stop. "I can't do it the way you do."

"Who says you have to?"

"Maybe you wouldn't have asked Rand what I asked. I'm beginning to understand that. We're twins, ReAnn, but we're different, too."

"Maybe more than I thought."

Julian leaned against his bike and watched a Monarch butterfly gather nectar from a patch of blue lupine. "Did Mr. Holland take the invitation?"

"Yes. He asked some questions, too. Before I left, he folded it and put it in his shirt pocket."

"I'm glad. I'm glad that you can do that sort of thing."

Later that evening, the family sat at the dinner table eating taco salad. The twins had agreed that Julian should bring up the subject of the kayak trip sometime during the meal. They would need their grandparents' permission.

As they ate, Grandpa talked about his plans for the house, what it was like when he was a child, and told a couple of humorous stories about the twins' father when he was a child. ReAnn glanced repeatedly at Julian as if expecting him to mention the kayak trip, but it wasn't until they were eating strawberry shortcake that her brother finally got to it. After he explained that they would rent kayaks at Pastor Bright's shop at Doe Bay and that they were planning a trip to Peapod Rocks with two brothers, the grandparents began asking questions.

"Is kayaking safe?" Grandma wondered, pushing her uneaten dessert toward the center of the table.

"No worse than riding a bike," Julian said, "and we won't have to watch for traffic."

"We'll be wearing flotation devices," ReAnn added reassuringly.

"The water is so cold," Grandma continued. "What about hypothermia?"

"There'll be four of us," Julian said. "We can help each other if there's any trouble."

"Who are you going with again?" Grandpa asked, a spoon of fresh strawberries hovering near his mouth.

"Rand and Jay Andrews," Julian said.

"Have I met them?" The berries disappeared, and the spoon dove toward the bowl.

"They were the boys we saw running toward the ferry yesterday," his grandson explained.

"The boys the sheriff warned us about?"

"They seemed friendly enough," Julian answered. "Besides, we're going kayaking. What trouble could we get into?"

"I'll tell you what," Grandpa said. "I'll talk to Pastor Bright. If he goes along with it, I'll agree. But you've got work to do first."

"Great!" Julian said.

Later that evening, Julian and ReAnn walked along the beach together, skipping rocks across the water. They leaned into a stiff breeze that pulled at their clothing and tussled their hair. Julian pointed out black cormorants, which rode low in the water with their heads pointed into the wind. ReAnn sighted a loon, and above the lone bird, barn swallows swooped over the water in search of insects. Her brother turned over a large rock, and they watched a handful of small crabs scurry for cover.

All the while he thought about the kayak trip. What would it be like on salt water? This evening the wind created whitecaps in the sound. Would there be whitecaps Thursday, and if so, would he get seasick? If he did, what would Rand and Jay say? What would they do if a pod of killer whales happened by? He hoped none of the creatures would crash into one of their kayaks. Remembering Rachael Falling Leaf, he wondered what she meant when she said that sometimes fear makes us blind.

The wind pulled at his shirt and whistled past his ears. A gull flew overhead, its head swinging this way and that. He followed the bird with his gaze until he saw Rachael Falling Leaf on the cliff above him. Her arms were outstretched, and her hair, now unbraided, blew in the wind.

CHAPTER 5

A Thief at Work

Sheriff Jordan drove down Grandpa's lane at 10:00 sharp the next morning. Julian was standing on the porch, a brush full of wood sealer in his hand. A small section of the porch around the door was all that remained of the deck to paint, and then he'd begin the railing. Grandpa pushed open the screen door and stood on the porch with a hammer in his hand. Climbing out of his car, the tall Black sheriff crossed the yard.

"You've done a lot of work on the old place," Jordan said.

"Just beginning," Grandpa said, stepping off the porch.

"Well, it looks good. Old Doc Brightwood used the house only during the summer. He'd drop his family off after school let out and pick them up at the end of August. Usually around the Fourth, he'd spend a week or so, fishing East Sound and sipping tea with other off-islanders at the Blue Pelican Resort. I guess physicians used to be able to do that back when they made money."

"What brings you out this way?"

"I talked to Pastor Bright about a meeting place

for that group you want to start. He said you might talk to him. He's the pastor of the Community Church, you know."

"Appreciate the lead, Sheriff," Grandpa said. "Could I talk you into a glass of lemonade?"

"Tempting, but I need to check on our camping public in the state park."

"Any problems?" Julian asked, remembering Cat Billet.

"No, just part of my rounds. I figure it's not a bad idea for the off-islanders to see we have a cop on duty. Maybe they'll behave themselves."

As the sheriff turned to go, Julian asked if anything new had turned up about the missing purse.

"The reappearing purse, you mean," the sheriff laughed. "No, nothing new. Too many other things to worry about." He ducked into his car and added, "The Freewalls haven't had any more trouble. I can't explain it, and I'm not going to waste more time trying to. Can't say the same for other people though. Seems as though islanders can't quit talking about it. Some think it's a miracle, and others think that trench-coated vagrant got scared and returned it. Who knows, maybe Mrs. Freewall just forgot where she put it."

He turned the ignition, and the engine started immediately.

"My car has been starting like this all morning," he said. "It's another thing I don't understand."

"Seems as though there's more than one mystery on this island," Grandpa said, smiling broadly.

"Maybe," the sheriff said, shifting into reverse, "and they're good ones for a change."

While they ate their lunch on the deck at the back of

the house, Julian noticed their elderly neighbor hobbling toward them through the woods.

"Mr. Holland, how nice of you to visit," Grandma called to him. "Can I fix you a sandwich?"

"I didn't come to eat," he said, breathing heavily. "I'm not going to make this trip often. It's just too much work." He sat on the bench.

Grandma poured a glass of lemonade and handed it to their visitor.

"Thank you." He lifted the glass to his lips, his hand shaking.

"Has it been a while since your last drink?" Grandpa asked.

"Twenty-four hours. An eternity. Does it make a difference?"

"None if you're not an alcoholic."

"You know I am." Mr. Holland took a deep breath and sighed. "I hadn't used the stuff in years until my wife died. Alcoholics Anonymous and my love for my wife kept me dry, I guess. When I lost her, I wanted to die."

"How about now?" Grandpa asked.

"I don't know." Pushing himself to his feet, he began his homeward journey. "Just wanted to return your kindness. The bread was thoughtful and mighty tasty, Ma'am. Thanks."

"You're welcome," Grandma said.

"Do you want to know about the study group when we get it going?" Grandpa asked.

"That would be fine. You're an Adventist, aren't you? Knew that because things change up here when the Sabbath comes around. I was raised an Adventist, you know. Lost track of it though. Had a lot to do with going into the Marines after high school. Different world there, I'm afraid." Mr. Holland stepped off the deck and made his way back into the woods.

"I think we have our first interest," Grandpa said. "We'll need to pray for him."

ReAnn beamed. Julian felt sure it was because she'd given him the invitation.

After lunch, Grandpa and Grandma drove to Eastsound to purchase lumber to repair the back deck. They also planned to talk to Pastor Bright at Doe Bay. The twins elected to remain behind, and an hour later, they found themselves at the edge of the bay.

Julian found a long kelp tube that had floated to shore, and pretending that it was a buggy whip, he snapped it. The end broke off and spun into the water.

ReAnn, who had been inspecting a crab the width of her hand, looked up when she heard the splash. Something in the distance caught her attention.

"We'll be doing that day after tomorrow," she said, pointing toward a kayak moving swiftly across the water along the far bank.

"I can hardly wait," Julian said. He noticed not a ripple disturbed the water.

"Who do you suppose it is?" she asked, approaching her brother.

"Hard to say." He snapped the kelp tube again. It made a satisfying pop. Another piece, smaller than the first, broke off.

The kayaker beached his craft and made his way up the bank.

"He must live there," ReAnn observed.

Julian glanced at the figure as it headed along the back

of a structure. A garage, he supposed. Just as he was about to ignore the person, something troubled him. He looked again, harder this time. "Maybe he doesn't live there," Julian said, dropping the kelp. He watched intently as the figure crouched at the corner of the building, and then slipped down the side of the building and disappeared. "Does that look like someone who lives there?" Julian asked.

"Looks like surreptitious behavior to me."

"Do you have to do that?" he demanded

"Do what?"

"You know perfectly well: use words no one else does."

"'Behavior' is a perfectly good word," ReAnn replied matter-of-factly.

Her brother groaned.

The figure reappeared and ran down the lawn toward the beached kayak. After stuffing something into the kayak, he pushed the craft into the water and began retreating up the bay.

"Let's go," Julian said and ran up the bank toward the house.

"Where are you going?" ReAnn asked, following her brother.

"To catch a thief. He just swiped something from the garage."

"What are you going to do if you catch him?" ReAnn asked when they reached the house.

"We'll figure that out if we do."

Locating their bikes in the front yard, they put on their helmets, jumped on their bikes, and raced down the lane. Once on the road, Julian shifted gears and leaned low over the handlebars to cut wind resistance. ReAnn fell behind as Julian pushed onward. Occasionally he caught a glimpse of the bay, but not once did he see the kayak. Was it headed toward town? Julian didn't know, but it was a reasonable guess.

Abruptly, the road rose over a small hill and dropped into town. Julian rode past the Blue Pelican and braked to a stop at the alley next to the bookstore. Dropping his bike, he ran down the alley onto the dock. The bay spread before him like a broad valley lined with green hills. A solitary fisherman, slumped over his fishing pole in a rowboat a hundred yards out, was all Julian could see. The kayaker was nowhere in sight.

Minutes later, ReAnn joined him. Stumbling onto the dock out of breath, she held her knees and gasped for breath. "Where do you suppose he went?" she asked finally.

"I don't know," Julian said, still studying the shoreline. "He probably got out of the water somewhere along the bank. Let's ride down the road and see what we can find."

"OK, but let's not make it an Olympic event."

Winding through town, the twins found the road that paralleled the eastern shore. Julian searched the side of the road for any sign of the kayak as they rode along. At times, the road ran close to the bay with a clear view of the beach, and at other times homes obstructed their view. In any event, Julian found nothing.

Finally, he stopped in a driveway. ReAnn pulled in behind him.

"I'm tired," she said. "Let's go home."

"Do you recognize this house and garage?" Julian asked.

"Should I?"

"I think it's where we saw the thief."

"You don't know he's a thief," ReAnn said, wiping sweat from her forehead. "You don't even know if anything's been stolen."

"I'm about to find out." Julian got off his bike.

"This is not a good idea."

"You don't have to come." He moved cautiously down the driveway.

"What if you're caught?"

"Bail me out of jail."

"That's not funny."

The driveway ended at the garage. The house sat to the left with a breezeway connecting the two buildings. A door about midway along the wall opened into the garage. A corner of the glass had been broken out. Julian tried the door. It was locked. Carefully he put his arm through the hole in the glass and unlocked the door. Stepping into the garage, he looked around.

A workbench lit by a large window ran the length of the building. It was littered with tools and fishing gear—the heavy gear of a commercial fisherman.

"Don't move," someone said behind him. "I've got a cellular phone, and the cops are on the way."

Julian swung around and saw a woman with ReAnn peering around her.

CHAPTER 6

A Thief's Work Continues

I'm not a thief," Julian protested.

"I know," Linda Phillips, the nurse, said and held up her hand. "Your sister explained it all. I can't imagine why someone would break in. There's nothing of value in here that I know of."

"Where did all this fishing gear come from?"

"My husband was a commercial fisherman. Owned his own boat. He fished salmon in the summer and rock bass and other bottom fish in the winter. This gear is just the way he left it."

"What happened?" ReAnn asked.

"We don't know for sure. He and a crew member left port on a cold March day six years ago and never returned. No trace of his boat was ever found."

"Oh," Julian said.

"I'm so sorry," ReAnn added.

"I've never really gotten over it, I guess, or else this junk would have been cleaned up. That's why I find it hard not to visit Mr. Holland occasionally. I know what he's going through."

"There was something here the thief wanted," Julian said. "He held it in both hands as he ran down to the water so it must have been heavy."

"Can't imagine what it would be," Mrs. Phillips said. "As far as I'm concerned, he can have it."

When Sheriff Jordan arrived, Mrs. Phillips and the twins were drinking glasses of ice water on the patio.

"It seems as though you two are in the middle of everything that has happened on the island lately," the Black man said as he walked up.

"We wouldn't be involved in this one," Julian said, "if we hadn't seen the thief at work."

"So you say." The sheriff pulled a spiral notebook from his shirt pocket and flipped its pages until he found a clean one. After making several notes, he asked, "Can you describe him?"

"Well," Julian began, "he ran fast."

"He crouched," ReAnn said, "and wasn't fat."

"Not fat at all," Julian added.

"He's thin, then," the sheriff said. "How much would you say he weighed."

"Hard to say. We saw him from across the bay."

The sheriff looked across the bay and considered the distance. "That's over a mile." He closed his notebook. "The fact that you saw anything is remarkable, but I doubt that you saw anything we can use."

"The kayak was blue," Julian said. "That should help."

"I think it was green," ReAnn countered.

"Green. Blue. Does it matter?" her brother asked. "How many kayaks are there on this island?"

"A hundred," the sheriff replied. "Maybe 200." He

stuffed the notebook into his shirt pocket. "I'd like to take a look at your garage, Ma'am."

"Certainly," Mrs. Phillips said.

The sheriff inspected the broken window first. Someone had smashed a corner out large enough for a hand and an arm to pass through. Cracks radiated from the broken corner across the window, and pieces of glass littered the floor of the garage. As they entered, it crunched under their feet.

Turning on the fluorescent lights, the sheriff carefully examined the workbench from one end to the other.

"What was here?" he asked finally, pointing to a rectangle neatly outlined by a coating of dust.

"It looks like something sat there for a long time and was recently removed," Julian said, leaning over the spot. "A car battery maybe?"

"I think it was a fish finder," Mrs. Phillips said.

"What's that?" ReAnn asked.

"A sonar device that tracks the location of fish beneath the boat," the sheriff explained.

"I don't know why anyone would take it," Mrs. Phillips commented. "It was old, and I'm not sure it even worked."

"The thief may not have known that," the sheriff replied.

"So," Julian began, gazing toward the ceiling as if deep in thought, "the thief has a kayak, blue or green, and some sort of boat, a skiff or larger, that up until now didn't have a fish finder. That should narrow your suspects."

"Most thieves sell what they steal for cash," the sheriff observed. "I think you should leave the detective work to me, son."

Offering the twins a ride home, the sheriff put their

bikes in his trunk. They were about to leave when ReAnn remembered she had an invitation to the study group in her pocket. She gave a copy to Mrs. Phillips.

"Thank you for inviting me," she said. "I have duties in my church. I meet Friday mornings with the parish committee. But you never know. I might show up. I don't have anything going on Saturday morning. I might just do that for no other reason than to encourage Mr. Holland. I think Father Trudeau would approve."

As the sheriff drove the twins home, he explained that shortly before Mr. Phillips had disappeared he'd reported unusual activities of several ships operating between Vancouver Island and Bellingham, the northern-most port in Washington State. "Some thought that smugglers had established a route by first dumping contraband on Vancouver Island and then moving it into the United States across the San Juan archipelago. It would be a simple matter. Vancouver Island has hundreds of miles of shoreline and most of it is wilderness. The Canadian authorities can't patrol it all."

"You think smugglers killed him?" Julian asked.

"I'm not saying that's what happened," the man answered. "I'm just relating one of the stories that still circulates around here. It beats the other one."

"What's that?" ReAnn asked.

"That he died in a storm."

Grandpa and Grandma were home by the time the sheriff arrived with Julian and ReAnn. Grandpa listened patiently as the sheriff explained what had happened.

"I believe their story," the sheriff concluded. "But is it more than coincidence that they've been in the middle of so many unusual events the last few days?" He looked first at Julian and then at ReAnn.

After he drove off, ReAnn said, "I've never been a suspect before. Do you suppose he believes we took the purse and then returned it?"

"Or that we broke into Mrs. Phillips' garage?" Julian added.

"Speak for yourself," ReAnn said. She headed for the house. "You were the one caught in the garage."

"Do you want to explain that?" Grandpa asked.

"ReAnn," Julian called. "Don't leave me now."

"It's your problem. Handle it." She bounced onto the porch and into the house.

The boy turned to his grandfather. "I suppose this isn't the best time to ask what Pastor Bright said about kayaking with the Andrews brothers?"

"No."

Around the supper table that night, Grandpa told of his conversation with Pastor Bright. The minister asked questions about the project and seemed interested. They agreed to meet later that evening at the church so that Grandpa and Grandma could see the facility. Although they had settled on nothing beyond that, Grandpa seemed hopeful. ReAnn decided to stay home and finish a book she'd been reading. "I've had enough excitement for one day," she said.

"What about the kayak trip?" Julian asked his grandfather.

Grandpa sighed heavily. "I'm not sold on the idea, but Pastor Bright said that of all the young kayakers on the island, he trusted the judgment and skill of those boys the most."

"All right!" Julian shouted.

"It seems strange to me that the sheriff tells us to avoid those boys, but the pastor tells us they're OK to kayak with."

After they had washed the dishes, Julian joined Grandma and Grandpa on the trip to the Community Church. The sun hugged the horizon as they drove into the church parking lot, and dusk was already gathering.

The church sat next to a wooded lot across the street from the Catholic church. Painted white with a tall steeple above the front door, the church appeared compact and old-fashioned. The gravel parking lot stretched from the front door of the church to the street with only a juniper at each corner of the building for landscaping.

They waited in the parking lot several minutes before Pastor Bright arrived. Grandpa slipped out of his pickup and shook the pastor's hand.

"This is my grandson, Julian," Grandpa said.

"We've met," Pastor Bright said. To Julian he added, "Heard you were caught in someone's garage today."

"Well . . . not caught exactly . . . " Julian felt his face turn color.

"It's still trespassing in my book," Pastor Bright commented. "Why didn't you call the sheriff when you saw what was happening?"

"Didn't think of it."

"Well, if it had been my home, I'd hope you would have thought of that first."

Pastor Bright took his keys out of his pocket, and Grandpa and Grandma followed him across the parking lot to the church. Feeling like he'd been stung, Julian hung back, leaning against the pickup. If he'd reported the incident and the kayaker had simply been the property owner retrieving something from his garage, Julian would have looked foolish. Now, however, he had made himself appear suspicious.

In the gathering dusk, Julian heard what sounded like footfalls on the rocky surface of the parking lot near the church. The pastor and his grandparents had already entered the building. Then he saw a shadow move swiftly across the parking lot and enter the woods.

Pushing himself away from the pickup, Julian jogged to the church, bounded up the steps, and entered the building. He found the pastor and his grandpa huddled at the rostrum.

"Why would someone steal PA cables?" the pastor asked. He held up a microphone. No cable was attached to it.

CHAPTER 7

The Accident

Julian watched the moonlight trace a path across his bedroom wall for what seemed like hours. He wondered how things could get so messed up in such a short time. Because of the incident at the garage, his sister wasn't speaking to him. Pastor Bright had scolded him when all he was trying to do was solve a mystery. Now he found himself withholding information. When Pastor Bright held up the microphone, Julian realized he'd seen the thief. The sheriff already thought it was more than a coincidence that Julian was always on the scene when something happened. If he reported what he had seen, it would only add to the sheriff's suspicions. Then there was the pastor. Already critical of the way Julian had handled the incident at Mrs. Phillips' garage, how would he react if he knew the boy had seen the thief running into the woods but hadn't alerted anyone? All this when his grandfather was trying to get permission to use the church.

Something else complicated the whole mess. When Pastor Bright reported the theft to the sheriff, he demanded that the officer do something about the vagrant. "When you allow down-and-outers like that on the island, you've got to expect trouble," the minister had said.

"What's your evidence he did it?" the sheriff asked.

"I'll tell you my evidence," the pastor said, throwing up his arms. "We had no trouble for months until the day that off-islander named Cat Billet arrived. Where did he get that name anyway? Since he walked onto the island, we've had nothing but trouble."

"We had plenty of incidents before Billet arrived," Sheriff Jordan said, "but it was mostly petty vandalism."

"Breaking and entering! Thefts!" Pastor Bright exclaimed. Holding up a microphone, the cable obviously missing, he added, "Crimes that result in a prison sentence."

Turning to Julian, the sheriff asked, "Son, would you say the man you saw running off of Mrs. Phillips' place was Cat Billet?"

"I don't think so."

"Why?"

"He didn't have long hair."

"Fine," Pastor Bright bellowed. "You're going to take the word of a kid who was over a mile away from the crime? I'll tell you how to handle this situation, Sheriff. Arrest that scum, and our problems will be solved."

Julian felt pulled in both directions. Pastor Bright made sense. The vagrant looked suspicious and may have been involved in some of what had happened, but Sheriff Jordan was also right. They had no proof. Besides, Julian knew how it felt to be a suspect when he hadn't done anything, and maybe the vagrant wasn't involved either. Still, something about the man made Julian more than uneasy.

When dawn broke, Julian, restless and unable to sleep, pulled himself out of bed, dressed, and slipped out of the house. A heavy dew moistened the grass, and he felt its cold wetness soak through his hikers to his skin.

A layer of fog hung over the bay and the air was still. A gull called in the distance, and another answered. Somewhere a splash sounded in the fog. *A fish must have jumped,* Julian thought. More sounds filtered through the fog as he listened: drops of water, the squeak of an oar lock, and something hitting the side of a boat.

The sun rose over the trees on the far side of the bay, and through the fog, Julian saw a figure in bold relief, back-lighted by the sun. At first the boy thought it was a fisherman, but as he watched, he noticed movements unlike those of a man fishing. The figure was throwing something into the water. Then Julian saw shapes surface on the water and slide under once again.

As the sun climbed higher, the fog slowly began to dissipate. As it did, Julian recognized the man in the boat. It was Mr. Holland. He was feeding seals from a skiff.

An hour passed before Mr. Holland turned the skiff toward his home. Julian met him on his dock and held the boat while the elderly man climbed out.

"Can't believe it," Mr. Holland said, straightening to his full height. "I looked out of the window this morning with my usual morning tonic in my hand, and I saw this boat tied to my dock. It's my boat, don't you see—the one that disappeared in a storm last spring. Look here. That's my number on the side. It's a little worse for wear, but seaworthy nonetheless."

"How did it get here?" Julian asked. The boat was wet both inside and out. Someone had scraped the wood, perhaps to remove barnacles, but the wood was sound. It had new oar locks, a new rope to secure it to the dock, and a set of oars, obviously used but in good condition.

"It's a gift." Mr. Holland knelt on the dock and ran his shaking hand over the gunwale. "I'd say it's been in the water for some time." Using the piling for support, he pulled himself back to his feet. "Don't tell your grandma, but I used the rest of the bread she gave me to feed seals this morning. They came right up to the boat . . . right up to the boat, just like old times."

After breakfast, Grandpa and Grandma assigned Julian and ReAnn to weed the flower beds in the front yard. They worked silently for some time. ReAnn chose to work on the opposite side of the yard from her brother. At mid-morning, Grandma brought out a pitcher of lemonade and two glasses.

"We need to talk," Julian said as they sipped their drinks.

"I don't think we have anything to say to each other," ReAnn said. "You've gotten us into enough embarrassing situations. I don't need that."

"I know. I apologize, but I've got something important to tell you. Two more things have happened. I couldn't tell you about what happened at the church last night, because you were already in bed when we got home."

"I don't want to hear it." ReAnn placed her empty glass on the porch, retrieved her hoe, and returned to work.

"Can I tell you some good news?" he asked, following her.

"I don't know." She slammed her hoe into a dandelion, popping the weed out of the ground.

"You'll like it."

ReAnn continued chopping weeds, and Julian thought she was going to ignore him, but finally she said, "OK, but that's it."

"Good. It's amazing. Mr. Holland got his boat back."

"What?" ReAnn paused in mid-swing.

"I couldn't sleep last night, so I got up early to see Mr. Holland's sea otters. Instead, I found him in his boat, feeding seals."

"I thought he lost his boat in a storm."

"He did, but someone brought it back." Julian watched her mutilate several weeds with her hoe with quick chops. "Do you want to know more?"

"Nope."

"Don't you wonder who is responsible or how it was done?"

"Listen, I couldn't be less interested. Why speculate? I'm glad for Mr. Holland, but I'm not about to get involved chasing mysterious figures all over the island."

Julian kicked at a dandelion with the toe of his hiker. Its white seeds flew into the air and floated on the gentle breeze over the lawn. "Me either," he said finally. "In fact, I want to forget the whole thing. Being a detective isn't as easy as I thought."

"Now you're making sense."

The boy returned to his side of the yard. Picking up his hoe, he asked, "How would you like to bike to Moran State Park this afternoon? Mountain Lake has a trail all the way around it. We could ask Grandma to make a lunch. It'd be fun. Besides, we need to make final arrangements with Rand and Jay for our kayak trip tomorrow."

ReAnn looked at her brother a long time before

answering. "I'll do it if you promise to forget about the mysteries."

"Didn't I say I would?"

"You said you wanted to."

"Small difference."

"A big difference to me." After a short pause, she added firmly, "Promise."

"Fine." He focused on a thistle, severing the stock from its root. The plant collapsed onto the ground.

"Well?" ReAnn persisted.

"Well, what?"

"I didn't hear a promise."

Julian whacked a morning glory into submission. Realizing his sister wasn't going to be satisfied with anything less than a promise, he said finally, "OK, I promise."

"Fine." She began hacking at another weed.

Grandma packed a lunch, and at noon the twins stuffed it into Julian's day pack along with two light jackets. After clipping a couple of water bottles to their bike frames, they pedaled down the lane. High clouds crept across the sky as they rode up the island, and by the time the twins reached town, the air had cooled and a breeze pushed against them from the north.

But Julian hardly noticed the weather change. Something at the back of his mind wouldn't let him enjoy his ride. He wished he hadn't made the promise to his sister, because he kept thinking of questions he'd like to ask the Andrews brothers.

Rand and Jay weren't visible as they approached the Blue Pelican Resort, so the twins turned into the parking lot. They spotted Rand washing down sidewalks at the back of the building. Leaving their bikes in the parking lot, they walked down the sidewalk.

"Hey," Rand said and turned off the nozzle. "Tomorrow's the day."

"Lookin' forward to it," Julian replied.

"And how about you?" Rand asked ReAnn.

"It should be fun."

"That's a marshmallow response," Rand said. "I expected to see some enthusiasm."

"Where should we meet?" Julian asked.

"Doe Bay is 10 miles from here. I'd suggest you have your grandfather drive you there and pick you up later in the afternoon—let's say at 5:00. We can meet at 10:00. How does that sound?"

"Sounds great."

"Bring a lunch and warm clothing in case the weather turns bad. It can do that quickly in the islands." He glanced at the sky. Julian looked too. The clouds seemed to be thickening. "You won't need an emergency kit. Pastor Bright supplies one with each kayak."

"We'll be there." Julian stared at the ground, considering his question. Then he looked at his sister. "I . . . uh . . . " He had promised himself a dozen times he wouldn't ask it, but now that he was here, he felt he had to. "There's something else," he said finally. "But it's not about kayaking." ReAnn put her hands on her hips and shook her head no. "ReAnn, I've got to. Just one question."

"Don't do it."

"Got to," Julian said, taking a deep breath. To Rand, he asked, "Do you know of anyone using a blue or green kayak on the bay yesterday?"

"Julian," ReAnn said with disgust, "you promised."

Rand looked puzzled. "What's she talking about?"

"That's it," ReAnn snapped, turning to leave.

"Wait, ReAnn," Julian called after her, following his sister. To Rand he said quickly, "Gotta go. Did you see anyone?"

"Don't think so."

"Thanks." Julian jogged backward. "See you tomorrow."

ReAnn turned her bike toward the road and threw her leg over the seat.

"Wait," Julian protested. Grabbing the back tire, he hung on to her bike.

"I can't trust you anymore. You're so obsessed by this mystery, you can't let it go."

"Why do you always have to do that?" he demanded more loudly than he'd intended.

"Do what?"

"You constantly use big words. 'You're so *obsessed* by this mystery.'" He mimicked her voice. "Do you do that just to make me mad?"

"No, I do it to irritate you. There's a difference."

Julian laughed so hard that he let go of ReAnn's bike.

"What's so funny?"

"Because you irritate me constantly with your million-dollar words, and I irritate you by being obsessed by this mystery."

"You don't irritate me. You make me mad."

"OK, Truce. I'm sorry."

"Sorry doesn't cut it."

"We're having a good time today. Let's not ruin it."

"You already have."

"OK. OK." He picked up his bike. "You can go if you like, and I'll return home with you, but I'd rather go to the lake."

Her shoulders slumped and she shook her head.

"I promise I won't do it again."

"Don't promise. Just don't do it."

Resuming their trip, the twins followed the road through the town and onto the eastern side of the island. The highway wandered through trees and around hills until they approached the park entrance. A log suspended over the road upon posts supported a sign that read "Moran State Park."

The twins coasted as the road descended to the lower lake. Dozens of campsites lined the shore, most filled with tents and a few with camp trailers. About midway Julian saw Cat Billet leaning against a tree. His back faced them, but his hair and oil-canvas trench coat were unmistakable. He watched as children threw bread to a flock of ducks. The man's black lab lay at his feet.

An ancient forest covered this part of the island. The trees rose high overhead and converged so that it seemed to Julian and his sister that they were riding through a tunnel. It was especially dark because of the clouds overhead. The weather had not improved, and Julian considered turning back and would have if they had not been so near their goal.

A sign at the end of the lake pointed to a road that ascended steeply into the trees. Mountain Lake, it said, was two and a half miles.

Julian shifted to the lowest gear as he turned onto the side road. His bike slowed, and he felt his calves tighten as he pushed his bike forward. The clatter from RcAnn's chain indicated she had shifted down, too.

Twenty tiring minutes later, Julian turned into the entrance to Mountain Lake. A short access road emptied into a parking lot fringed on several sides with trees and the lake on the other. It was immediately clear that the weather had turned nasty. Cloud cover obscured Mount Constitution. A mist, coarse and heavy, had begun to fall. In minutes, moisture layered the parking lot, and droplets, which formed on leaves and fir boughs, fell to the ground, making plopping sounds.

After leaning their bikes against a tree, Julian drained a bottle of water.

"Do you suppose we're in for a storm?" ReAnn asked finally. "Maybe we should head home."

"Probably will rain," Julian said, glancing into the sky. "But I'm hungry. Let's eat and then decide what to do."

Julian pulled the two jackets out of the day pack and gave one to his sister. ReAnn unzipped the collar pocket and pulled out the hood. Slipping into the jacket, she extended the hood over her head.

Finding a relatively dry spot under a grove of cedars along the shore, they sat down and opened their lunch.

"Umm, cheese sandwiches," ReAnn said, lifting the corner of Grandma's homemade bread.

Julian chomped down on a carrot stick. "Nothing like the outdoors to make food taste its best." He stared out on the lake. An old-growth forest lined the opposite shore and was reflected in the clear waters of the lake. The wind they had fought earlier had died down, and for now, the only sound was the moisture dropping off the trees.

"I'm sorry for bringing up that stuff with Rand," Julian began.

"Don't even think about talking about it," ReAnn hissed, raising her hand.

"You've got to know one thing," Julian persisted.

"Boy, you don't give up, do you." She turned her back to her brother.

"Pastor Bright told the sheriff last night he wanted Cat arrested."

"Why?" ReAnn demanded, facing him.

"When we got to the church, we discovered someone had taken all the PA cables. The pastor was angry and was sure Cat was responsible. 'The scum . . .' He used that word. 'Arrest the scum and our problems will be solved.' He said that."

"He did?"

"Something like that."

"That doesn't make sense. Why would a man like him need PA cables?"

Julian scooted toward his sister and lowered his voice. "He'd sell them," he said, remembering the sheriff's statement. "Cat needs money, not cables. Makes sense, doesn't it?"

"And who's going to buy them? Tell me that."

"I don't know. Someone needing cables."

"I'm sure he'll find one of those on every street corner," ReAnn said dryly.

The mist had turned to rain. The lake danced as droplets of water struck its surface. Overhead, rain pelted the tree, and in minutes the moisture made its way through the tree and fell on them in large drops. Water streamed off the asphalt parking lot to the gutters along the curbing. But something else held Julian's attention. Something dark. Something coming their direction.

"Let's go," he said suddenly. Jumping to his feet, he stuffed the remainder of the lunch into the day pack.

"It is getting worse," ReAnn observed. Holding her palms up toward the descending rain, she watched the droplets collect on her skin. "Maybe we should go home."

"We need to go now. That stranger is coming this direction."

ReAnn looked over her shoulder. Cat Billet was bent over his handlebars and straining up the last slope at the entrance of the parking lot, his trench coat pulled high over his neck. His black lab trailed at his rear wheel, its red gums in a permanent snarl.

ReAnn jumped to her feet and used a tree to hide from the man. Julian, however, watched as Cat rode into the parking lot. Water beaded and ran off his oiled canvas coat. His wet hair hung in strings along the side of his bearded face. As he passed, his head turned, and Julian looked into his eyes and saw only black lifeless holes in a face that had no expression.

"Now!" Julian commanded after Cat had passed by. They dashed to their bikes. Julian pushed his helmet onto his head and turned his bike toward the exit.

"Go, go," he yelled, letting his sister lead the way. Over his shoulder he watched Cat who turned his bike in a tight circle and headed toward Julian.

Julian peddled for all his worth. Shifting up and straining into the pedals, he gained on his sister. Rain soaked his clothing. His tires cut through the water on the asphalt.

"Faster," he yelled, sure the man was gaining on him.

At the exit, he barely looked for traffic as he shot out of the parking lot and passed his sister onto the road. On down the hill he flew, gaining speed at an alarming rate. Rain pelted his helmet and spattered against his face, which made it difficult to see. He dropped his head against the rain.

Hurtling around the first corner, his wheels slipped on the wet pavement. Frantically he corrected, nearly losing control. Another corner approached at lightning speed. He depressed the hand brakes with all his strength, but water on the pads made them useless. Realizing too late that there was nothing he could do, he leaned into the corner. His front wheel lost traction, and he felt himself going down. Tucking in his shoulder, he tried to prepare for the collision. As he slammed into the pavement a searing pain knifed through his body, and he tumbled helplessly, wedged into his bike, until he and the bike flew off the road and into the air.

Hopelessly entwined in his bike, he hit the ground with a bone-shattering crash. Then bouncing free from his bike, he rolled and finally came to rest, arms and legs splayed in every direction.

At first he was sure he was dead, and then as the pain settled into his body, he wished he were. On the road above him, he heard his sister's bike squeal to a stop. Several hops down the steep bank and ReAnn reached her brother's side.

"Where does it hurt?" she asked.

"Everywhere." He moaned.

"You!" someone above them shouted. "I've seen you before."

Julian lifted his head to look. Towering over him was the dark shape of the man in a trench coat. The black dog also looked down at him, something slimy and thick drooling from its muzzle.

With a groan Julian dropped his head to the ground.

CHAPTER 8

The Stranger

Cat slid down the bank and crouched over Julian. Throwing his hair over his shoulder, he ran his hand up and down Julian's limbs, checking the bones. He asked what hurt. Julian couldn't locate anything specific except for the side of his body that had first hit the pavement.

"You're lucky," Cat said finally. "Nothing seems to be broken. See if you can climb up to the road."

As Julian struggled to turn over, it triggered more pain. While he crawled up the hill, Cat went after Julian's bike.

When at last all three stood at the edge of the pavement, they looked over the bank. Crushed fern indicated where Julian had first hit the ground and where he eventually ended up.

"Anyone speeding down this road in this rain must be crazy," Cat said angrily. "Don't you know you could've killed yourself? If you'd flown through the air another several feet either direction—splat! You'd hit a tree, and someone would've carried you out of that ravine. It wouldn't have been me. I don't carry jerks who voluntarily kill themselves. Look at your bike. Imagine that wheel was your head." The front rim was badly twisted.

"It's not that I meant to lose control," Julian replied weakly, rubbing the ache in his side.

"He was afraid," ReAnn said, crossing her arms.

Julian shot her a look that could have killed.

"Afraid of what?" Cat demanded.

"That's a bit complicated," ReAnn said, "but he was afraid of you."

Julian rolled his eyes, grabbed his bike, and began walking it down the road.

"Why me?" he heard Cat ask.

"There has been a whole series of mysteries since we arrived, beginning with the stolen purse aboard the ferry."

"I see, and I've been linked to them?"

"You've been suspected."

"No evidence but suspected anyway. Where's the American principle of innocent until proven guilty?"

"Look," Julian interrupted, "it's raining. I mean raining hard. I'm wet, cold, and sore. My bike is wrecked. And we're about two miles from cover. Can we get out of here?"

"Sure," Cat said. "Just trade me bikes for a minute."

Using the quick release hubs, Cat removed Julian's damaged wheel. He then released the hubs on the back wheel of his bike and adjusted the spacer nut wide enough to insert the forks of Julian's bike. After moving the brake pads out of the way, Cat inserted Julian's forks onto the axle of his bike and tightened the hubs.

"It'll sort of be like riding tandem: a bicycle built for two," Cat said. "Sort of."

"That's pretty neat," Julian said.

"It will be if it works," Cat said. He strapped the bent wheel to his pannier. "The trick is, you can't steer and I can't pedal. But it's all down hill. You're sort of the trailer—you're just in it for the ride. Get on. We'll take it slow and easy."

Fifteen minutes later, Cat pulled into the ranger station at the edge of the camping area along the lower lake. He and ReAnn found shelter under a canopy over a picnic table while Julian placed a call to his grandfather inside the ranger station. When finished, he joined his sister and Cat.

"Grandpa said he'd be here in a few minutes. He thought we'd be calling, because of the rain."

"Did you tell him about your accident?" ReAnn swung her legs back and forth at the end of the picnic table. Cat sat on the table too but rested his feet on the bench.

"Just that my wheel is bent, and I can't ride it."

"I thought you rode it just fine," Cat said. "I just don't intend to take you all over the island, especially in this rain."

"What are you?" Julian asked. "An engineer or something? That was a nifty thing you did with the bikes."

"Close. I'm an electrical engineer with a specialty in chip technology."

"You're on vacation, right?"

"Sort of. A long one. I have a wife—or had a wife—a house, two cars in the garage, a dog, and three children. It's all someplace—it's all gone."

"I'm sorry," ReAnn said.

"Well, it was my fault. Something went wrong while I was on my way to the American dream. After I'd spent a year of 16 to 18 hours a day working on product development, my wife left me. She said it wasn't fun anymore."

The black lab shook water from its fur and placed its chin on his master's foot. Cat reached down and patted the dog on the head.

"When she left, it wasn't fun for me anymore, either. So I left my work, and a year or so later, I ended up here with old Raven, still looking for something I lost." The dog looked up at his master, his red tongue hanging. Cat rubbed the dog's neck.

"Raven?" Julian asked. "Where did he get that name."

"He's black just like the bird in Edgar Allen Poe's poem about the raven. 'Quote the raven, Nevermore.' Sort of seemed appropriate." Cat reached into his pocket, pulled out a scrap of food, and fed it to his dog. "We were hit by a car last winter. That's where I got this scar." He pointed to a ragged line that crossed his cheek. "Raven got the worst of it. He lost an eye and something happened to his saliva glands. They seem to be working all the time." A string of slimy substance hanging from the dog's jaw slung this way and that as the animal ate the treat.

"Did you take Maggie's purse?" Julian asked. He sat on the bench.

"Julian!" ReAnn exclaimed. "After all this, how could you ask?"

"It's all right," Cat said. "I didn't know it was missing until the purser questioned me aboard the ferry."

"How about the PA cables at the Community Church?"

"I can't believe you're doing this," ReAnn said with disgust.

"Is everything that's missing on the island going to be blamed on me?" Cat demanded.

Raven paced his head on Julian's lap, and the boy

ran his hand through the dog's wet fur.

When Grandpa arrived, Julian, ReAnn, and Cat told about the accident. Cat replaced Julian's wheel and helped get the bikes into the pickup. The damaged wheel rose above the pickup bed, twisted and useless. All Julian could do was shake his head.

After Grandpa talked for some time with Cat he finally invited him to the first Sabbath meeting. Grandpa told him it would meet at 10:00 in the morning at the Community Church.

"I'll be there," ReAnn said to encourage him. "I'll be looking for you."

"It might be nice to meet with friendly people," Cat commented.

As they drove away, he waved and watched them until the pickup reached the park entrance.

"You got permission from Pastor Bright to use his church?" ReAnn asked.

"Not yet," Grandpa said, "but we've got to launch out in faith. The board of deacons are to meet soon and decide the matter."

"Is that a good idea?" Julian asked. "What happens if you can't use the church?"

"The Red Sea parted only when Moses walked to its shore and spread his hands over the waters. What would have happened if Moses refused to walk to the sea until the waters were already parted?"

Julian wasn't sure. He'd have to think about it.

As they passed through town, Julian wished his bike's twisted wheel were buried under ReAnn's bike. Instead, it stuck into the air like a beacon for all to see. Julian was glad he didn't see either Rand or Jay as they drove past The Blue Pelican.

When they arrived home, Julian pulled his bike out of the pickup and threw it onto the front lawn. Fixing it would require a trip to a bike shop, and he didn't remember seeing one on the island. He would have to ask Rand and Jay if Friday Harbor had a bike shop.

After changing into dry clothes, the twins sat at the dining-room table and sipped hot chocolate that Grandma had prepared. Rain pelted the deck as they told their story. Grandma clicked her tongue on the roof of her mouth when she heard about Julian's brakes failing, and Grandpa shook his head as the boy explained how Cat had solved the bike problem.

Finally the story wound down.

"I completely forgot," Grandma said after a few moments of silence. "I had a visitor this afternoon who left a package for you, Julian." She retrieved a box from the kitchen counter and handed it to Julian. "Rachael said this was for you."

Pushing his empty cup aside, he placed the box on the table in front of him and broke the cellophane tape seal. Opening the lid, he pulled back the white tissue to reveal the clay orca fired with a deep blue glaze.

Turning it over in his hand, he admired its smooth surface and rich detail. On the bottom Rachael had inscribed a message in the clay before she had fired it. It read, "Fear makes us blind. Faith makes us free." Julian placed the sculpture on the table and leaned back in his chair. The animal appeared to be forever caught in a leap from the waters of the sea.

CHAPTER 9

Peapod Rocks

Julian awoke at 8:00 the next morning. He was immediately aware of two things: the stream of sunshine that flooded his room—the storm was over—and that every move of his muscles resulted in painful agony.

Sliding out of bed with a groan, he unfolded his body slowly and tested his muscles. Shuffling into the bathroom, he inspected himself in the mirror. Ugly purple bruises covered his thigh and shoulder.

After getting dressed, he hobbled into the kitchen and poured himself a glass of orange juice. Sitting in a chair on the deck, he drank and let the warmth of the morning sun penetrate his body. It looked as if it was going to be a perfect day for the kayak trip—not a breath of wind, and that meant calm waters. He worked his shoulder, trying to loosen the muscles.

ReAnn loped up the hill.

"Mr. Holland saw the sea otters this morning," she declared as she jumped onto the deck. "He said they chattered to him just like in the old days. He thought they were glad to see him."

"I've been thinking," Julian said.

"That could be dangerous." ReAnn settled into a chair next to her brother and fanned herself with her hand.

"Do you suppose Cat Billet simply told us a good story? Maybe one he's practiced over time."

"Julian Hunter, you're the most suspicious person I've ever met. And you would have to be my brother."

"Just thinking of all possibilities."

"What about the possibility that he's telling the truth?"

"That's the other possibility."

"You know what I think?" ReAnn asked, leaning forward. "I think this has all been caused by aliens. Or leprechauns? Or ghosts? How about ghosts? Is that a possibility?" Her brother didn't answer. "I think I'd like a glass of orange juice. Excuse me." Pushing herself out of her chair, ReAnn disappeared into the house. While pouring her juice, she yelled back at him, "Maybe it's like Mr. Holland's sea otters."

"What about them?"

"They don't really live around the islands. He believes they do because he wants them to." ReAnn returned with her drink. "Maybe you're seeing a number of unrelated things, and you're thinking it's all from one individual because that's what you want to believe."

Grandpa appeared from around the house. "Pretty good job, Julian," he said as he stepped onto the deck.

"We weed to please," Julian said, referring to the previous day's work in the shrubbery beds. He drained his glass.

"Well that too, but I was referring to your bike. The bent wheel is about as true as a new one."

The twins looked at each other and said at the same time, "Ghosts."

When they gathered around Julian's bike, they could see that Grandpa was right. Julian lifted the front of the bike off the ground and spun the wheel. Only a slight wobble remained.

"Someone had to work pretty hard on those spokes in order to take the twist out of the wheel," Grandpa observed. "I've tried it and know it's not for someone who has no experience."

"Cat could have done it," Julian said. He looked at his sister. She merely shook her head.

At 10:00 Grandpa turned into Doe Bay. Rand and Jay waved as Grandpa stopped in front of Pastor Bright's kayak shop. Four bright fiberglass kayaks sat on the lawn at the side of the building with gear stacked next to them. The brothers were packing it into the kayaks. A trail behind the building led down the rocks to an inlet. Julian watched the water. Swells, gentle and deep green, sloshed along the rock walls of the inlet.

Shaking off a rolling sensation in his stomach, Julian followed his grandfather into the building. Kayaks, canoes, snorkeling gear, and scuba equipment covered the floor, shelves, and counters. Nautical maps, some yellowed with age, hung on the walls.

After helping another customer, Pastor Bright greeted them. "Got your paperwork ready to go," he said. "Just need your signature and a payment."

Julian placed several bills on the counter. Pastor Bright returned the change.

"This is a safe activity, isn't it?" Grandpa asked.

"About as safe as it can get. The weather report is for

perfect weather—clear with no wind. Each kayak contains emergency gear, including waterproof walkie-talkies with fresh batteries. My radio is always on and ready for a signal. Rand and Jay already know where they can go, and they know the safety rules. I think your grandchildren are in for a perfect day."

"Don't worry, Mr. Hunter," Jay said, entering the store. "It's a lot safer than cycling."

"Funny you should mention that," Grandpa said. He glanced toward Julian who happened to be rubbing his hip.

Jay gathered an armload of gear and said, "Dozens of bikers were injured on the island last summer, but not one kayaker was hurt unless you count sunburns." He left the building.

"Well, just take care of yourselves, you two," Grandpa said. He mussed Julian's hair.

"About the church," Pastor Bright said, "I regret that the board of deacons voted not to let your group use it."

"I'm sorry," Grandpa said. "It's a good project, worthy of your backing."

"Likely," the minister commented. "It was a matter of principle, however. If we let your group, we'd have to let others. This way, we don't have to worry about precedent."

"Is there anyway the deacons might reconsider?"

"The decision is final. But I'll be praying that the Lord will open up something for you."

"Thanks, I appreciate that." Disappointment clouded Grandpa's face. Turning to Julian, he said, "I'll be here at 5:00."

After Grandpa left the store, Julian asked, "How many deacons are there on your board?"

"Three," Pastor Bright said.

"Who's in charge?" ReAnn asked.

"That would be Mike Jordan. Why do you ask? By the way, the PA cables are back."

"Oh," Julian said.

"Whoever took them repaired the fraying cables. Most unusual." Pastor Bright frowned.

"It *is* amazing," Julian said dryly. "Do you still think Cat Billet did it?"

"That's what we've got a sheriff for," Pastor Bright said as he examined a sheet of paper on the counter. "He'll figure it out and take the appropriate action."

"If the cables were returned, then maybe it's like Mrs. Freewall's purse," ReAnn suggested.

"What do you mean?" the minister asked, glancing up from his paper.

"No crime was committed," Julian added.

"Oh, there was a crime, all right," Pastor Bright snapped. He dropped the paper into a wooden box marked "Possibly Important." "Someone broke into and entered the church twice. That's two counts of 'breaking and entering.'"

"Snazzy question," Julian whispered as he and ReAnn left the store. "You're getting gutsy. Not bad."

"He made me mad," ReAnn said. "And Sheriff Jordan is behind it all. Can you believe that?"

"Just because he's the chairman of the board doesn't mean he was responsible for the way the vote went."

"Well, I intend to ask him," ReAnn sputtered, stabbing the air with her outstretched finger.

"Now, that's more like it," Julian said. "Maybe we're more like each other than we thought. We just champion different issues."

"Champion?" ReAnn asked bewildered. "Where do you get such words."

Julian laughed in spite of the stab of pain it caused.

Before placing their kayaks into the water, Rand and Jay instructed the twins on the use of the double-ended paddle.

"It's a single handle," Rand explained, "held with both hands. With it, you turn the kayak." He demonstrated how to accomplish a turn. The twins mimicked his actions. Rand also showed them the correct technique to propel the craft forward.

"And," Jay continued, "if you capsize, this is how you right yourself." Turning the end of the paddle so that it would be flat to the surface of the water, he moved it in a semi-circular motion.

The twins practiced the technique until the brothers were satisfied with their efforts.

"We're not planning to capsize today," Rand said, "but if it should happen, remember you have a couple minutes to get it back into an upright position. If you can't do it using a paddle, you can slip out of the kayak and swim to the surface."

"Right," Julian said, but he didn't feel as sure as he sounded.

"The next trick is getting into the kayak," Rand continued. "We'll use a protected beach. Once you get used to the paddle, we may head for Peapod Rocks."

"You'll love it," Jay said. "Kayaking is a snap."

Thirty minutes later, Julian and ReAnn were beginning to feel comfortable with their new skills. Paddling caused Julian's shoulder to ache, but his hip felt fine once he settled into the kayak. After practicing in the calm water, Julian began to feel as if he wasn't going to get motion sickness. But everything changed when they left the shelter of the cove. Immediately Julian felt the slight rise and fall of the water under him. Though gentle, the motion as well as the rocking of the kayak as he paddled sent his stomach rolling. It took all his concentration to keep the waffles he'd had for breakfast in his stomach.

The Andrews brothers led them along the shoreline. They pointed out areas of interest as they passed. "The meanest dog on the island lives there." "We've never seen anyone at that cabin. Maybe it's haunted." "That house belongs to Albert Barnes. He used to work for military intelligence."

"Intelligence?" Julian echoed. He recalled the story of smugglers and Mr. Phillips' disappearance. "Are you sure?"

"Of course," Rand said. "He goes to our church. Barnes said the Russians used to run their submarines to the edge of the archipelago and sit on the bottom."

"Maybe one is underneath us right now," Jay suggested.

Julian looked into the deep blue water but could see nothing.

"Used to happen all the time," Jay continued.

"I remember jets sweeping out of the sky and dropping stuff into the water," Rand said.

"Mr. Barnes said they'd drop torpedoes just to let the subs know they weren't getting away with anything," Jay explained.

"Torpedoes?" Julian asked.

"Dummy torpedoes."

"Did he ever say anything about smugglers?"

"No," Jay answered.

"There are probably smugglers around though," Rand said, "but Mr. Barnes doesn't know anything about them."

"Do you?" Julian asked.

"Sure," Rand said.

"No," Jay said.

"I mean, I've heard people talk," Rand said. "But I haven't seen any."

"Me either," Jay added.

"I wouldn't want to," Rand said.

Jay grimaced. "Probably too dangerous. They wouldn't want people to discover who they are."

"I've heard they don't take prisoners," his brother said.

"What does that mean?" Julian asked.

Rand ran his finger across the flesh under his chin.

"They'd kill us?" ReAnn asked.

"Or worse," Jay replied. "People do desperate things when they don't want to be discovered."

"I see," ReAnn mumbled.

"Like return something they'd taken?" Julian asked, referring to the purse.

"It would throw off suspicion," Rand suggested.

"It would create confusion," Jay said.

"That doesn't make sense," Julian protested. "Why would someone steal something and then risk getting caught by returning it?"

"Some things are not what they seem," Rand declared. "Mr. Barnes said that one time they dropped torpedoes and the sub didn't move. When the navy checked it out, they discovered that what they thought was a sub, wasn't a sub at all."

"What was it?" ReAnn asked.

"A dummy. The Russians had pulled a dummy sub

all the way across the Pacific Ocean to the archipelago."

When they were directly across from Peapod Rocks, they turned away from the island and paddled into the open water. Julian wasn't sure which was the greater problem: his aching shoulder or his jumpy stomach. Near the island, a kelp bed spread before them, its long fronds floating in the tide like strands of hair.

Rand and Jay took their paddles out of the water at the edge of the kelp.

Looking over his shoulder toward Orcas Island, Rand observed, "If you were standing on the beach on the island, you wouldn't be able to see us."

The trees above the shoreline were clearly visible, but the horizon hid the beach from view.

"Another mile and you wouldn't be able to see us even from the base of the trees. You could yell, scream, and wave your arms and no one in the houses would see you."

"I don't like that," Julian said.

"Perhaps they could see you from the mountain," Rand said, "but who'd be looking?"

A swell lifted under Julian's kayak. His stomach rose, too. Something slammed against the side of his craft, bouncing him violently. The water around him boiled. Icy spray splashed over his kayak and onto his body. The taste of salt water filled his mouth.

"That was close," Rand said. "Is everyone OK?"

"What happened?" ReAnn cried.

Julian wiped the water from his face and realized he'd dropped his paddle. He looked around for it and saw instead a massive gray shape moving away from him through the water. A geyser blew into the air from the whale's airhole.

"It's a gray," Jay yelled with excitement in his voice.

"It's going down," Rand said.

The whale's head dove into the water, and its body followed until its tail flew into the air and disappeared as well.

"What an entrance!" Jay declared.

"A little too close for my comfort," Julian said. His paddle floated just beyond his reach.

"The whale came through the channel between the rocks, I think," Rand mused. "That's why we didn't see it as we approached."

"They do that," Jay said. "At high tide sometimes."

"Is that so?" Julian reached for his paddle. The kayak tipped. "You could've warned me."

"Guess so," Rand said. He slapped the water next to the floating paddle and sent it bobbing through the water toward Julian.

Julian took the paddle and backed his kayak away from the kelp. "We're a little close, aren't we?"

"Where's the whale now?" ReAnn asked.

"We won't know until it breaks the surface," Rand said.

"How long do they stay down?" Julian asked, scanning the surface of the water.

"Until they run out of air," Jay told him.

The gray whale exploded out of the water at the far edge of the kelp bed. Waves rolled under the thrust of its body.

Julian held his breath and wondered where the whale would surface next. Would it be beside his kayak or under it? Would the whale come up under his sister?

Julian paddled backward, moving his kayak away

from the kelp bed. Something bitter moved up from his stomach.

"It'll follow the edge of the kelp," Rand said.

"You're going the wrong way, Julian," Jay warned.

"Where should I be?" Julian asked, feeling panic.

ReAnn had already moved into the kelp bed and continued toward the island. Rand followed close behind her.

"You'd better get moving," Jay urged.

Julian plunged the paddle into the water and pulled forward. His shoulder rebelled, and the bitter fluid seeped into his mouth. He gagged as he forced it back down. Another couple of thrusts of his paddle, and his kayak slipped into the kelp bed.

Behind him, the gray whale shot out of the sea, its long body flying into the air. Water sprayed in every direction, and a wave washed over Julian's kayak, rocking it violently and giving him a thorough drenching. The broad side of a gray whale filled his vision. Julian's mouth fell open in awe of the magnificent animal, and at that moment, the whale plunged back into the sea. Another spray of water descended upon Julian and filled his open mouth.

The motion of the wave coupled with the biting taste of salt water was more than his stomach could take.

CHAPTER 10

Fire on
the Hearth

"Y"ou should have seen it, Grandpa," ReAnn said, once they were on their way home. She was so excited that she nearly shouted. "It was the most beautiful thing I've ever seen."

"How did you like sighting the whale, Julian?" Grandpa asked.

"I'll never forget it," Julian replied, only now beginning to feel he was gaining control of his stomach.

"I didn't hear any whale song," ReAnn said thoughtfully. "Did you, Julian?"

"Not that I remember." Now that he thought about it, all he could remember of the first few minutes was his terrible fear and being sick.

"Its breathing, though," ReAnn said, back up to full volume, "was loud. I mean l-o-u-d."

"That I do remember well," Julian said. Recalling Rachael Falling Leaf saying that sometimes fear makes one blind and deaf, he wondered what his fear had prevented him from noticing that day.

As they passed through Moran State Park, they saw Sheriff Jordan's car parked next to Cat Billet's camp. The sheriff had Raven's head pinned to the pavement with the heel of his boot, and he was handcuffing Cat.

Grandpa pulled to a stop behind the cruiser. Julian jumped out of the pickup and knelt before the dog. The sheriff removed his foot, and Julian put his arm around the dog's neck. The animal growled.

"What's happening, Sheriff?" Grandpa asked.

"Should be pretty clear," the sheriff said. "I'm arresting this man for breaking into the bookstore on the night the purse was returned."

"I thought you said no crime had been committed," Julian said, smoothing the fur along the dog's neck.

"As far as I'm concerned there was no crime with regard to the purse," Jordan said. He guided Cat toward the cruiser. "But the break-in is another matter. Linda Phillips reported seeing Cat hanging around outside the building late Sunday night when she was returning from a late night visit."

"How did she know it was Cat?" ReAnn asked.

"He's the only man on the island with a trench coat and a black lab," the sheriff said. He opened the back door of the cruiser, placed the flat of his hand on the back of Cat's head, and eased him past the doorpost. "Like I said, nothing was taken from the store, but breaking and entering and trespassing are still crimes in Island County. It's my job to make sure the island is safe."

Billet hung his head in the back of the car.

"Did you do it, Cat?" Julian asked.

"Yeah, sure. I'm going to break into a bookstore and return a purse I didn't take." He shook his head in frus-

tration. "I was only hungry. So was Raven. I was checking out the garbage cans in the alley. There's a restaurant there, you know."

"I know," Julian nodded.

Grandpa volunteered to take care of Cat's belongings
until the issue was resolved. "How about Raven?" Cat asked.

"There's an animal shelter in Friday Harbor," Sheriff
Jordan said. "I'll see it gets there."

"No," Julian interjected. "I'll take care of him."

"Fine with me." The sheriff slammed the car door
and climbed in behind the wheel. "About Cat, I just take
them in," he said apologetically. "It's up to the judge to
sort it out."

"What about the church?" ReAnn asked.

"What about it?" Jordan asked.

"Why did you vote not to let Grandpa's group use it?"
Her voice was strung tighter than a violin string.

"What she means to ask is," Grandpa interrupted,
"would you reconsider? If we could just use the church
until we find another place . . ."

"Talk to the pastor. Now, if you'll excuse me . . ." He
drove off, the cruiser's tires spinning in the dirt at the
edge of the asphalt.

While Grandpa and Julian collapsed Cat's tent,
ReAnn collected the few camping articles strewn
around the camp: a hand mirror, several nesting pots, a
few wilted vegetables, and a small hatchet. When
Grandpa put Cat's bike into his pickup, Raven jumped
onto the bed and wagged his tail.

Later that evening, Julian and ReAnn filled an old
washtub with water on the deck. "Do you suppose Raven
will let us give him a bath?" ReAnn asked her brother.

"I think he'll do anything for a treat. Come, Raven." He held a Gravy Train nugget in the palm of his hand.

Raven wagged his tail and inched closer, eying the tub warily.

"Come on," ReAnn coaxed. She patted the soapy water as if that would encourage the dog to jump into the tub.

Julian held out his hand, and Raven lapped up the morsel of food. While the dog chewed his treat, Julian heaved the animal into the tub. "Go for it," he said, feeding the animal another nugget.

ReAnn poured a bucket of soapy water over Raven's front shoulders. The dog ignored the water and continued to eat.

Grandpa stepped to the door, a phone to his ear. "I'm not asking for a permanent arrangement, Pastor. Just four weekly meetings, that's all."

As ReAnn soaped down the dog's fur, Raven sniffed Julian's hand for another treat.

"I just need a little time to find another meeting place," Grandpa continued.

ReAnn moved to the dog's head. Raven licked at the suds with his tongue and rolled his head. "Better give him another one," she said.

"How soon will I know?" Grandpa asked.

"I'm all out," Julian told his sister.

Raven stretched toward Julian. "Sorry, dog," the boy said, backing away.

"Friday night is awfully late," Grandpa said, "but if that's the best you can do . . ."

Scooping up another bucket of water, ReAnn poured it over the animal's back.

Raven jumped out of the tub, planted his paws squarely on the deck, and shook his body, beginning with his shoulders and ending with his tail. Soapy water sprayed in every direction. Grandpa ducked into the house. Julian jumped back, slipped on the wet deck, and landed on his seat, water dripping from his face. ReAnn stood, gasping, "Oh, my. Oh, my."

"Never thought you'd lack for the big words," Julian commented. He wiped his face with his T-shirt.

ReAnn smiled and brushed soapsuds off her blouse.

His tail whipping the air, Raven sniffed at Julian, waiting for another treat. Cords of saliva, hanging from his jaw, danced around his muzzle.

That night Raven slept next to Julian's bed. Some time after the moon rose and its light filled Julian's room, a sound awakened the boy. At first disoriented, he thought it was cloth ripping, but as his mind cleared, he realized the terrible noise was coming from Raven. The dog was snoring. Julian lay back on his pillow and wondered if it was another problem caused by the accident Cat had mentioned. He reached down and patted the dog's thick body.

The next morning Grandpa announced at the breakfast table that they would not work on the house today. "I printed a hundred invitations last night," he said, "and I want to hand them out all over the island."

"Sounds fun," ReAnn said enthusiastically.

"About as much fun as running a sliver under a fingernail," Julian muttered under his breath.

"What about a meeting place?" ReAnn asked, scowling at her brother.

"We've been praying that God will work something

out," Grandpa said. "Now it's time to act as if we believe He will."

"I know," Julian said. "Like Moses."

"That's about it." He handed a flyer to Julian. "We're going to see what happens as we step out in faith."

Julian read the flyer. "Meet at the Community Church parking lot," it read.

"Too bad you can only take three of us in the pickup," he said, not feeling bad at all.

"This is voluntary," Grandpa replied. "You don't have to go. Maybe you could see that Rachael gets an invitation while we're gone."

The house seemed empty after everyone left. Julian sat sullenly on the deck, watching the waves play on the sound. Raven lay at his feet, occasionally scratching behind his ear. The invitation Grandpa had given him had blown off the table and lay somewhere behind him on the deck. "I know Rachael already received one," Julian remembered his grandfather saying. "But this new one tells where we're meeting." It made sense, but it seemed a waste of time.

The morning sun danced off the waves. A breeze whispered in the trees overhead, and from somewhere, a gull cried. *Do orca whales ever enter East Sound?* Julian wondered. He thought of the clay figure Rachael had given him and finally decided he wanted to thank her. Maybe he'd give her the invitation at the same time. If he wanted to, that is.

Julian pulled himself off the chair, found the invitation, and headed up the hill. Raven trotted at his heels, sniffing at the forest floor along the way.

As the boy topped the bluff, he checked out

Rachael's work area first, but she wasn't there. The table was empty. No clay. No remnants of any recent work.

Raven sniffed at the air and growled.

"It's OK, boy," Julian said, running his hand along the dog's neck.

Circling the cabin, Julian stepped onto the porch and knocked at her door. No sound came from inside.

Again, Raven barked, startling the boy. Julian looked toward the bluff. The work table was out of sight. Then he glanced toward the lane that dropped sharply through the trees to the road. Nothing. Finally, he looked through a window into the house.

Smoke filled the room!

Now that he'd seen it, he could smell it.

He pressed his face against the glass for a better look. An orange flame licked along the floorboards in front of the hearth.

Fire!

Julian beat on the door. Still no answer.

Jumping off the porch, he grabbed a rock and shattered a window next to the door. Behind him Raven barked excitedly. Reaching through the broken window, Julian turned the dead bolt. Then throwing open the door, he entered the house. The flames had already spread and now towered halfway to the ceiling.

Finding the kitchen, he turned the water on in the sink and threw open the cupboards, looking for a container. The smoke bit at his eyes and caught in his throat, making him gag. Coughing wildly, he held his stomach and fought for control.

Turning back to the cupboard, he found a large bowl and put it under the tap. Below the oven in a drawer, he located a kettle. Back at the sink, he replaced the over-flowing bowl with the kettle.

Stumbling toward the living room, he threw the water at the base of the fire and returned to the kitchen for the kettle.

Back and forth. Each trip was more difficult than the last. The smoke thickened, which made breathing even harder and finally near impossible.

By now he lost track of the number of trips he had made between the fire and the sink, but he couldn't stop. Even though his head swam from the lack of oxygen, he had to make sure the fire was out.

Stay near the floor.

He'd heard that somewhere. A teacher? Fire safety drill? Colliding with the counter, he fell to the floor.

Throw water at the base of the fire.

Hadn't he done that?

He thought so.

Call 911 and leave the building.

It made sense. Why hadn't he done that?

Something pulled at him. Tugged at his sleeve.

Julian jerked his arm free, but again something grabbed him. He moved in the direction it pulled him. Whatever it was it yanked harder. Then growled.

The dog, Julian thought.

Crawling now, Julian headed blindly across the floor. Smoke and steam filled the room until his eyes watered so that he could see nothing. His lungs ached, and his head swirled.

At the door, he pulled himself to his feet and stumbled onto the porch. Leaning over the railing, he wretched, coughed, and finally gulped fresh air into his lungs.

Raven pushed at his leg with his wet nose, and Julian reached down to rub the dog's neck. "Good fellow," he said as the animal licked his hand. For once, Julian didn't mind the saliva that dripped from the dog's mouth.

After Julian managed to find the phone and call 911, he sat on the porch and waited for the fire department to arrive. A siren wailed from somewhere near Eastsound and minutes later the fire engine drove up the lane. The fire fighters chopped into the pine flooring and put out the remaining hot spots.

One gave Julian oxygen, and Sheriff Jordan, who arrived several minutes after the firemen, asked questions. Rachael drove into the yard about the time the firemen were putting away their equipment.

"So," she began, sitting on the porch next to Julian after she looked at the damage, "you're the one who has been creating all the mysteries."

"Just this one," Julian replied. He briefly recounted how he had discovered the fire and had attempted to put it out.

"I'm very grateful," she said. "My house would have been only glowing coals by now if it hadn't been for you."

"Thank you for the orca figure," he said. "That's why I came—to thank you."

"I'm glad you liked it."

Julian rose to go and then remembered the paper in his pocket. He reached for it. "Oh," he said slowly. "My Grand . . . I mean . . . I brought you an invitation to the study group meeting on Saturday. This one says it'll be at the Community Church." He handed it to her.

"So, you were here to thank me and to invite me to this meeting?" Rachael Falling Leaf asked with a smile spreading across her face. "Two more good things."

"I suppose so." Something warm seemed to settle into his chest, and it felt good.

CHAPTER 11

To Catch
a Thief

As Julian walked slowly through the trees toward his grandparent's house, he thought about the woman's words. "My house would have been glowing coals . . . ," she'd said. Elijah had poured water on an altar, and a fire from God had burned it up. In a small way, Julian felt he'd done something similar. Like Elijah, fire and water were involved. But Julian had used water to put out a fire. It wasn't quite Elijah's miracle, but he decided it was no less a miracle from God.

He remembered his fear and confusion in the smoke, and he wondered just how he had been able to hit the flames with the water. He couldn't have done it on his own.

What if he'd chosen to do nothing? Obviously, the flames would have destroyed Rachael's house. How did he know he could make a difference? He didn't, of course. In fact, he hadn't even considered it. It was like ReAnn and her efforts to share her faith. She didn't stop to consider whether she could make a difference—she just did it and left the results to God.

An idea began to form in Julian's mind. Maybe Grandpa hadn't considered all the options. Was there something else that could be done about finding a temporary meeting place?

Surprised by the sudden change in his thinking, Julian began jogging toward the house. The taste of smoke still filled his mouth, and its smell clung to his clothing. In spite of the pain in his hip, he shifted into high gear, and his feet flew along the forest floor. He imagined that he was outrunning the smoke, leaving it behind among the trees. The cool morning air filled his clothing and chilled his face.

Once in the house, Julian drained three glasses of water and then filled Raven's bowl to the brim. While the dog greedily lapped at the water, Julian thumbed through a phone directory, looking for Linda Phillips' phone number. But he found no listing for her.

Having already made a decision to talk to her, he determined to follow through with his plan. Locating his bike, he headed down the lane with Raven trotting alongside. Once on the asphalt, Julian shifted into cruising gear and headed up the bay.

As he passed the resort, Julian looked for the Andrews brothers, but they weren't in sight. The sheriff's cruiser was parked in front of the jail, and it reminded Julian of Billet. That was another problem. How was Cat going to get out of jail?

Once through town, Julian turned onto the road that paralleled the eastern shore. Behind him Raven's nails clattered against the pavement, and he heard the dog's pace quicken as Julian put his weight into the pedals.

His hip ached with each thrust, and his shoulder burned as he leaned onto the handlebars, but he ignored his discomfort and pedaled all the harder.

At Linda Phillips' driveway, Julian slid to a stop behind her red Geo Metro, jumped off his bike, and dashed to her front door. Pressing the doorbell, he waited impatiently for an answer, but no sound came from inside the house. After the second ring, he gave up and ran around the house to check the backyard. Still no sign of her.

Raven growled.

"What do you see, boy?" he asked. The dog nudged his leg. Julian looked around. The house and garage rose behind him on the hill. The lawn, bordered by trees and brush on both sides, fell away in front of him to East Sound. Then he saw it. A kayak, green—green like ReAnn had remembered—rested on the beach.

Immediately thinking of the garage, Julian sprinted around the house to the door with the broken window. The door was closed but unlocked. A piece of cardboard, taped over the hole, had been torn free and hung loosely.

Julian opened the door, then hesitated before entering. His eyes adjusted slowly to the darkness. Looking behind the door, and into the corners of the garage, he soon satisfied himself that no one was lurking in the building.

Knowing that the thief must be hiding somewhere, Julian returned to the backyard only to discover the kayak missing. The thief had eluded him again.

He retraced his steps to the driveway, jumped on his bike, and headed back up the road. Around the first corner, he caught a glimpse of the kayak through the trees. It sped along the shore.

Julian struggled over a rise in the road, around a corner, and then down a hill. The road wandered away from the water at this point, and Julian lost sight of the kayak. Raven fell behind. Slowing, Julian called, "Come on, boy."

The road whipped back toward the bay. The kayak had continued to pull away, but if Julian remembered correctly, the road straightened from here to town so he would have an excellent chance of overtaking it.

He began to pedal harder, and Raven continued to fall further behind. Clearly, the dog was tiring.

A car sped around the corner ahead of him. Julian hugged the edge of the road and slowed his bike. As it passed, he recognized the passenger: Mrs. Phillips.

Glancing at the kayak, Julian applied the hand brake and skidded to a stop in the gravel. He hit his handlebar in disgust and watched as the kayak disappeared behind a stand of trees.

Raven stopped at Julian's side and sat down, his tongue dragging the ground.

"I'm sorry, old dog," the boy said. "I guess it's not that important we catch the kayak anyway."

He emptied the contents of his water bottle into the palm of his hand, and the dog lapped up the liquid. Then Julian turned his bike toward Mrs. Phillips' home and glanced only once over his shoulder in the direction he'd last seen the kayak.

"Well, Julian!" Mrs. Phillips said in surprise as she answered the door. "Don't tell me there's another thief about."

"Another kayak, at least," he said simply. "Before I explain, I'm dying of thirst. Could I have some water?"

"Certainly," she said, opening the door wide.

Julian and Raven followed her down the hall into a

bright kitchen. A bay window above the sink looked out on the water, and an oak table sat in front of a floor-to-ceiling window that shared the same view.

Mrs. Phillips turned on the tap and opened the cupboard to retrieve a glass. "Now tell me what happened," she said as she tipped the glass under the tap.

"I got an idea," Julian began. He watched the water swirl in the glass as it filled. "I tried to call you, but your name isn't in the phone directory."

"I live alone. Perhaps it's a foolish precaution." She handed the glass to Julian, who took it and drank it all in one gulp. "An article in a woman's magazine said that a woman living alone should have an unlisted number." Taking a bowl from the cupboard, she filled it for Raven.

"May I have another?" Julian asked, handing her the glass. He emptied the glass twice more as he explained the circumstances that had brought him to her house. "I thought for sure you'd be here. Your car was in the driveway."

"It usually is on Friday mornings. A friend down the road always gives me a ride to my committee meeting. It gives us time for a friendly chat."

"You do that every Friday morning?"

"Without fail. Well, if I'm not sick or something."

"Whoever broke into your garage knew that," Julian said. He placed the empty glass on the counter. "I guess that eliminates off-islanders, doesn't it?"

"You lost me," the woman said.

Julian explained how he had seen the kayak as he circled the house looking for her. "I immediately thought of the garage," he said, "but no one was there. When I returned to the backyard, the kayak was gone. I took off down the road and saw him ahead of me, but that's about the time I spotted you."

"Why did you give up the chase?"

"For two reasons," Julian said. "I wanted to see what he took this time, and I wanted to talk to you about something."

"Well, first things first. I'd like to see what he took, too."

The two walked down the hall through the breezeway into the garage. Mrs. Phillips switched on the fluorescent lights, and together they scanned the workbench.

"Is that it?" Julian asked, pointing toward a black box with a small TV-like screen sitting on the corner of the worktable.

"The fish finder!" Mrs. Phillips exclaimed. "Someone brought it back."

CHAPTER 12

Turn
of Events

Thirty minutes later after discussing his plan with Mrs. Phillips, Julian continued his trip toward town. Raven, having recovered, trotted at the edge of the road. The kayaker was nowhere to be seen, but then Julian didn't expect the thief would still be on the bay. He watched the shoreline nonetheless for any sign of the kayak.

At the edge of town, he parked his bike and descended to the beach. The head of the bay was only a half a mile long, and most businesses that lined the shore faced the street. A rocky shoreline was accessible to the public with the exception of an area under a retaining wall that ran behind the central businesses of the town, which included the bookstore and restaurant. They had been built directly above the water at the top of a retaining wall. A solitary pier knifed into the bay between the bookstore and restaurant. You could reach the pier from the alley.

Julian and Raven followed the beach until they

reached the retaining wall. The beach disappeared at this point, and a waterline on the retaining wall marked high tide. The tide was out.

Not able to go farther along the beach, Julian jumped to the top of the retaining wall, which at that point was only several feet above the beach. Making their way between the buildings, he and Raven came out on the street.

"You wait here, Raven," Julian ordered as he opened the heavy wood door that lead into the bookstore. The dog curled up against the wall next to the door and began panting. The bell above the door rang as Julian entered the store.

"Hi," Allie said, emerging from around the end of one of the bookshelves. "ReAnn with you?"

"She's handing out invitations with Grandpa." He walked between the bookshelves toward the back of the store.

"To that meeting on Saturday?" Allie followed at his heels. "We got one, too. What is it, anyway?"

"It's a Bible study group." Julian passed the unoccupied checker board and wished the pastors had been playing chess. They would have been in an excellent position to see something out the window. "Are you coming?"

"I don't know. Maybe."

"I hope you do." He stood before the window that looked out on the water. "Did you see a kayak on the bay today?"

"No."

"Have you seen a green kayak on the water at anytime?"

"I don't particularly remember a green one. I've seen kayaks out there sometimes, though."

"But not today?"

"That's right."

"Well, when you saw a kayak, do you remember where it came to shore?"

She studied him. "Why are you so interested in kayaks all of a sudden?"

"Just wondering."

Allie joined him at the window and looked out over the water. The retaining wall was just below them and the water below that.

"I don't ever remember seeing a kayak come to shore at this end of the bay," she said. "Maybe down the beach but not here. I've seen one from time to time off the end of the pier, but that's as close to the shore as it comes." She pointed out the window. "Why would someone take a kayak into town?"

"I don't know, but when I do, I think I'll have solved the mystery."

"What mystery?"

"Who took the fish finder from Mrs. Phillips' home and returned it again. And maybe even brought your mother's purse into your store."

"That would be nice," Allie said, looking out the window with new interest. "But didn't the sheriff already arrest someone for breaking into our store?"

"Yeah," Julian replied, "but Cat didn't to it."

"How do you know?"

Julian thought about her question for a moment. How did he know? Was it because the facts didn't add up? It was more than that, he decided. "Because I know Cat," Julian said finally. "He wouldn't have done it."

Satisfied he'd gathered all the information he could

from her, he left the bookstore. Kneeling beside Raven, he ran his hand along the back of the dog's neck as he considered his next move. The kayak couldn't just disappear, he knew. It had to be somewhere.

Turning down the alley, Julian decided to take another look at the bay. The pier was empty, and as Julian walked onto its weathered planking, the boards moaned and popped under his weight. The crescent-shaped beach was empty except for several seagulls scolding each other over the possession of a dead crab.

Raven sniffed at the planking near where it intersected with the retaining wall, then growled and scratched at the wood.

"What is it this time?" the boy asked.

Raven looked off the dock and barked.

Julian knelt beside the dog and looked down along the retaining wall. He expected to see water, but under the shadow of the dock he saw rock covered with green seaweed. Steel bars in the shape of stair steps descended along the wall at the edge of the dock. Though rusty, they looked sound.

Cautiously Julian climbed down while Raven whined and paced along the retaining wall. As the boy worked his way toward the rock fill, he felt the coolness of the ocean on his skin, and a confusion of smells assaulted his nose, including creosote from the dock and salt and vegetation from the sea.

Raven barked—a high-pitched bark of excitement—and flung himself off the wall. He landed with a splash in the cold bay water and paddled toward Julian. When he reached the rocks, he shook the water off his fur.

Julian turned away from the spray and scrambled to

the top of the rock under the dock. It was dryer there. No seaweed. The rock apparently was above the high tide mark. Julian ran his hand along the concrete wall and looked into the shadows along the underside of the dock. Then he saw it. Suspended by a set of pulleys and ropes was the kayak. It hugged the underside of the dock.

Raven growled as he sniffed along the rocks.

"You suspect something, too?" Julian asked without expecting an answer. "Who do you suppose uses it?"

Raven continued sniffing at the rock along the base of the wall. It apparently had been placed as fill under the dock, perhaps to protect the wall or the dock against erosion, Julian decided.

Inspecting the kayak above him, he saw that it appeared well used. Instead of the highly polished plastic of Pastor Bright's kayaks, this one looked as if it had been homemade with a coarse fabric stretched over a wood frame and then painted green.

As his eyes got used to the shadows, he noticed a hole in the retaining wall just behind the kayak. Grabbing the edge of the opening and pulling himself up, he rested on his arms, then looked into the hole. To his surprise, it was a culvert of some kind. Steel bars ran vertically from the ceiling into the floor, but years of moisture had eaten the metal away. Now the bars were pushed to one side, leaving an opening large enough for someone Julian's size to slip through.

Scrambling into the opening, he eased himself between the bars and into the belly of the culvert. First he crouched to get his bearings. His hair brushed against the ceiling, and he could touch the side of the culvert with his fingers. Then he crawled slowly into the darkness.

It amazed him how quickly silence and darkness engulfed him. Raven's bark sounded hollow and distant beyond the opening. From somewhere ahead came the steady drip of water. Otherwise, he heard no sound except for the scrapping of his hikers along the moist floor of the culvert.

For a second Julian considered turning back, but it seemed as if someone, perhaps the person who used the kayak, was using the culvert. If Julian was right, maybe that person was still in there somewhere.

He checked his progress by glancing at the opening behind him. It grew steadily smaller as he moved deeper into the culvert.

A movement in the air brushing the side of his face alerted him that he'd come to a junction. Pausing, he listened. From somewhere in the distance voices murmured, and Julian turned toward the sound.

The new tunnel was smaller, and he had to crawl on his stomach. He moved quietly but deliberately along the cement. The voices grew louder but were still indistinct, partly because they seemed more like whispers and partly because of the echo effect inside the culvert. Then a faint sliver of light materialized before him, and he edged toward it.

The voices fell silent. Then came soft laughter, finally hushes.

Julian reached toward the light, and his hand touched a barrier in front of him. Its rough texture told him it was wood of some sort. The sliver of light penetrated through a small crack in its surface.

Stretching toward the crack, he tried to peer through it. All he could see was a flicker of light. The voices began talking again.

Inching his way forward, he pressed his face against the wood, hoping to get a better view. Someone or something moved between the flicker of light, and for a moment, he saw a shape. Placing the flat of his hands on the wood, he squinted into the hole.

Without warning, something touched his leg. In fright, Julian jumped, his shoulder hitting the wood barrier. A snap was quickly followed by a crash, and he found himself tumbling out of the culvert onto a floor.

Before him sat two boys, eyes wide, with a candle on the table between them. Above him, standing in the mouth of the culvert with his tail wagging, was Raven.

"Where did you come from?" Rand asked. He stood and brushed his hair back with his hand.

"Well," Julian began, "I was looking for whoever was using the green kayak this afternoon." He brushed the dust off his pants. Raven jumped out of the culvert and began sniffing around the earthen floor.

"That would be me," Rand said.

"How did you know to look here?" Jay asked.

"I wouldn't have," Julian said, "if it hadn't been for Raven."

"Well, he's a smart dog," Jay nodded.

"What is this place?" Julian asked.

"Your guess is as good as ours," Jay replied. "I think it was once used as a cool room for storage."

"Or for smuggling," Rand suggested.

"But it's a perfect place for us," Jay added.

"I guess," Julian said. "I was lucky to have found it."

"You're not going to spoil it for us, are you?" Rand asked.

"I don't see why I should," Julian said. "But I would

like to know a few things. Like, was it you who returned the fish finder?"

"Yeah, I did. Took it as well. Didn't want to break the window, but there was no other way."

Julian looked puzzled. "Why?"

Rand held up his hand. "First things first."

"The sheriff doesn't think much of us," Jay said matter-of-factly. He leaned his elbows on the makeshift table. The candle, stuck in the end of a bottle, flickered.

"I noticed," Julian said.

"For good reason," Rand said. He picked up the plywood Julian had knocked from the culvert and slipped it back into place in front of the opening. "We've done, let's say, a few pranks."

"Most not the kind of stuff that could be pinned on us," Jay said, "but then who else could have done it? Jordan knew all right."

The candle flame grew steady and cast long shadows on the concrete walls.

"Stuff like the graffiti on the sheriff's office, I suppose?" Julian asked.

"Yeah, and soap in the resort's hot tub," Rand said.

Julian's eyebrows rose. "I didn't know about that one."

"That one got us 30 hours of donated labor," Jay grimaced. "We could have paid a fine, but my dad said we'd have to work it off."

"Is that why you were working at the resort?" Julian asked.

"At first," Jay said. "But they liked our work and hired us. It's not a bad job really, and we like the money."

"We weren't too smart about that prank," Rand said, "but it worked out well. We were thinking of another one, a big one, when we found Mrs. Freewall's purse on the ferry."

"Then we thought," Jay added, "wouldn't it be fun if the purse mysteriously returned rather than us giving it back?"

"It was easy as pie," Rand explained. He waved his hand around him. "As you can see, we're below the bookstore."

The earthen cellar was no larger than Julian's bedroom. Overhead was the floor of the bookstore. Julian could hear the squeaking of the boards as people moved around above them.

"There's a crawl space under the rest of the store," Jay pointed over his shoulder, "and over there is the access into a closet upstairs. It was a simple matter to sneak the purse into the store when everyone was gone."

"Simple," Rand agreed.

"Did you think of that as trespassing?" Julian asked.

"We were returning a purse," Jay said. "Who would complain?" He shrugged.

"What about the fish finder?" Julian asked.

"Wait, that isn't all," Rand said. "Remember how the sheriff had to crank the starter on his car to get it started? We sneaked into his yard early one morning and changed his spark plugs. The guy never maintains his car."

"You fixed the PA cables, too?"

"Yeah," Jay said, "and your bike rim."

"How did you know about my bike?"

"Rand was in the alley when your Grandpa drove by," Jay said. "It was easy after that."

"What about the fish finder?" Julian asked again.

"That's the best one," Rand said. "We wanted to find Mr. Holland's boat."

"We like the water and knew how we'd feel if we lost our kayak," Jay added. "We had heard about his skiff sinking in a storm last spring. But we needed some way of finding it. The fish finder outlined the bottom of the bay. It was just enough to show us where the skiff was."

"We used a grapple hook to pull it up," Rand explained.

"Did you ever think it was stealing to take the fish finder?"

"We didn't plan on keeping it," Rand said. "It was too bad I had to break the window to get into the garage."

"We sure got the town buzzing," Jay laughed.

"Yeah, you did," Julian nodded. "But most people still don't know it was mostly good things that you were doing. They see only the bad like breaking into the store to return the purse and breaking into the garage to use the fish finder."

"Well, that wasn't our plan," Jay said.

"Yeah," Rand added, "and they were all supposed to be good things we did. It was to be different, not like the dumb stuff that got us into trouble."

"Something else happened," Julian said. "Something you didn't plan."

Rand stared at him. "What's that?"

"Cat Billet was arrested for breaking into the bookstore," Julian said. "The sheriff thinks he stole the purse and then returned it, because he was afraid he'd be caught."

The brothers looked at each other. Jay shrugged. "I don't see there's anything we can do about that. We're out of good-prank ideas."

"Maybe you've done a lot of things without thinking about the consequences, whether good things or bad,"

Julian said. "Sometimes what you've done has helped people, but right now Cat is sitting in jail for no reason. Maybe your best prank will be to figure out a way to get him out of jail."

For a moment both boys stared at Julian, and then they got to work, thinking up a new plan.

CHAPTER 13

The Parking Lot Meeting

The pink light of early morning filled Julian's room when he woke on Sabbath morning. The house was silent. Raven sprawled on the floor next to his bed and let out several muffled barks. Dreaming, Julian decided. The boy turned over and thought about the events of the last week. It had all been exciting, but now most everything had been solved. The mysteries anyway. Two things remained: the need for a meeting place for Grandpa's study group, and what was going to happen to Cat.

Pastor Bright had called Friday night and said the deacons had refused to reconsider letting the study group use the church even for only four weeks. It looked as if the Community Church was not the place they would meet. Grandpa said they'd have a parking lot meeting instead. He'd find some place by next Sabbath.

Julian was about to fall asleep when he heard the sound of an oar strike the side of a boat. Pulling himself out of bed, he looked out the window. A splash of color stretched across the eastern horizon, promising a clear sunrise. Through the trees, he glimpsed Mr. Holland's boat. It looked as if the old man was on his way into the bay.

As Julian dressed, Raven woke, stretched, yawned. Together they crept out of Julian's room and into the kitchen. The boy took his grandfather's binoculars from the dining room table and left the house. Instead of descending to the beach, he climbed through the trees to the bluff where he knew he'd have a perfect view of the bay.

"I don't expect visitors so early," Rachael Falling Leaf said as Julian joined her at her work table.

"And I didn't expect to see you working so early," Julian replied.

"It's the light." Rachael's fingers worked a shapeless mound of clay. "It's different at this time of day." The material seemed to melt into hills and valleys at every touch. "What brings you out from the warmth of your bed at this hour."

"I heard Mr. Holland," Julian explained, remembering why he'd climbed the hill. Lifting his binoculars, he watched as Mr. Holland rowed gently toward the southeast near a kelp bed.

"Is this the first time you've watched him?"

"This early." Julian marveled how Mr. Holland dipped the paddles in and out of the water without a sound. "He seems to love the animals."

"He's got the heart of an Indian," Rachael said. "But a love for this planet and the creatures that live in it is in everyone's heart, if we'd just pause long enough to listen."

Under her touch, the clay was beginning to take the graceful shape of some living creature. Julian wasn't yet sure just what it was going to be.

Through the glasses, Julian followed Mr. Holland's progress. The old man finally pulled the oars out of the water and let the boat drift, and then the boy saw a movement on the surface of the bay. First one creature and then another broke through the water, turned, dove, and resurfaced.

"I don't believe it," he exclaimed.

"Nothing is impossible," Rachael said. "Especially for those who believe and have patience."

"Did you know?"

"Of course. That's another reason I'm here. Mr. Holland's love for those creatures calls them to this bay."

The clay in her hands had taken a final shape. Only the details remained, but it was clear that Rachael had captured the shape of a sea otter in her clay—Mr. Holland's guest.

Shortly before 10:00, Julian, his sister, and Grandpa climbed into the pickup. Raven jumped into the box. Grandma said she'd wait at home and pray for a successful meeting.

As Grandpa turned into the Community Church parking lot, several people had already assembled. Rachael Falling Leaf and Allie waved at them. Behind them stood Mrs. Freewall and a man Julian didn't know. Others milled about in a small group, talking.

Grandpa slid out of his pickup and walked over to them. "This'll be a parking lot meeting," he announced. "I'm sorry for the inconvenience."

"It's a good day for it," the tall man standing next to Mrs. Freewall said. "My name is Jim. I'm Maggie's husband." His wife put her arm around him and smiled.

A car turned into the parking lot, and Mr. Holland got out. "I'm not too late, am I?" he asked.

"Not at all," Grandpa said, holding out his hand.

"Well, I had something to do before coming," Mr. Holland said. "I buried my last whiskey bottle at the bottom of the bay. That stuff's killing me."

"I was just telling everyone that we have no place to meet, so we're going to have our meeting here this morning."

"Fine with me," the elderly man replied. "You could meet at my home, if you like."

"That's a fine invitation, but because this is a Christian group, I was hoping to have the cooperation of a church, but I see that may not work out."

Yet another car pulled into the parking lot. Father Trudeau stretched and walked toward them. "A fine group you have here," he said. "Morning all."

Various greetings came from the crowd.

"I talked to Mrs. Phillips on the phone last night," Father Trudeau said as he shook Grandpa's hand. "She said she'd talked to Julian about your need for a place to meet. Sounds like a worthy cause, and there is always a need for a new fellowship for believers. My church is open to you all if you want to use it."

"That's a fine thing for you to do," Grandpa said. "We accept the offer. I don't think it'll always be such a fine day for an outdoor meeting."

They crossed the street to the Catholic church. The priest opened the front door and showed them a room in the basement they could use. As they moved chairs into a circle, someone else entered the room.

"Excuse me," Sheriff Jordan began, "but it seems as if I've been mistaken about a few things." He explained how he'd discovered a new coat of white paint on the outside walls of his office that morning. "And," he continued, "two boys were sitting on the steps, waiting to explain a few things. Turns out they'd been doing good pranks for a change. We're so used to thinking off-islanders are responsible for what we don't like or understand that we were ready to accuse an innocent man. Anyway, Mr. Billet is free to go. The charges will be dropped. I've brought Mr. Billet here at his request. He said he wanted to be with your group."

Cat Billet walked into the room. He had washed his hair and fastened it back with a rubber band, and he wore a clean shirt.

"I'd like to meet with you, if it's all right," he said.

"Of course," Grandpa said, beaming.

Later, after the meeting, Allie, ReAnn, and Julian sat on the front porch of the church while the adults talked about their plans for more sessions. Raven lay at their feet, licking his paw, and Allie stroked the dog's fur.

"Just think," ReAnn said. "A few days ago, I thought Raven was the ugliest dog in the world."

"He scared me," Allie added. "I thought he looked mean."

"I think he scared us all." Julian patted the dog. "His injury made him look that way. I guess you can't always tell about a person or a dog by the way he looks."

"You mean Cat too," Allie said.

"Especially Cat." Julian remembered how he had fled from the man on his bike and how it had led to an accident.

"I don't know how you did it, Julian," ReAnn said. "Somehow you solved the mysteries, got Cat out of jail, and found a church to meet in."

"It was easy," her brother explained. "You just have to believe in what you're doing."

"I guess I learned something, too" ReAnn said. "We have different talents for a reason."

"Well, remember that the next time I ask for help with physics." Julian rubbed Raven's ears and the dog moaned and his back paw scratched at the air.

"If I can get your help with history," ReAnn said. She touched the bridge of the dog's nose with the tip of her finger.

"Plan on it," Julian announced.

The dog licked the back of ReAnn's hand, but when ReAnn noticed a strand of saliva hanging from the bottom of the dog's jaw, she jerked her hand away.

Julian laughed.

"What's the deal?" ReAnn asked, backing up a step away from the animal.

"It just struck me as funny," he said, letting the dog lick his hand. "As twins, we're the same, and we're different at the same time, and that's OK."